FIND
FIX
FINISH

a novel by
Jeremy Brown

For Ellen

A tremendous thanks to Bryan G. Wilson, US Army Special Ops (Ret), who was an inspiration and amazing, constant source of information for this book. Any technical/operational accuracy is because of him—the mistakes are mine. When I asked Bryan how he'd like his name displayed, this was his only request:

God Bless America

CHAPTER 1

"WAIT, WHERE ARE your guns?"

Darwin looked at the other people walking out of the El Paso airport, some of them glancing over to see what this guy was talking about. Marty Lindy was standing next to a dark blue Suburban, his hands out like if he didn't like the answer, Darwin and his team were going back on the plane.

Darwin lifted the black Pelican lockbox, the size of a thick briefcase. "Right here. Nice to meet you, Mr. Lindy."

Marty stared at the case. The client file said he was in his mid-fifties. Up close, he'd had some work around the eyes.

"That's it?" Marty looked at the older man standing next to him. The guy looked comfortable wearing a suit in the Texas heat. Marty said to him, "Dave? I thought this was taken care of."

Darwin stopped, Cal and Gabe on either side, and waited. He wanted to see how Marty handled it. It was uncomfortable, a guy twenty years older than him about to throw a tantrum, but they were used to it from clients. Cal scratched that beard of his, watching all the El Paso cowboy hats walking around.

Dave put his fingers together in front of him and said, "We think there might be a need for more than that."

Darwin set his bag down, kept the case in his left hand.

"Dave, nice to meet you. Patrick Darwin." They shook hands, Dave a little embarrassed. "We have more coming, just got held up coming out of Baghdad. One of us'll come up tomorrow and grab them."

"What kind are they?" Marty asked.

"The kind that fire bullets."

Marty's eyebrows went up, not used to the sass, and Darwin stuck his hand out. Marty looked at it, then over at Dave. He shook Darwin's hand and said, "Goddammit Dave. This kid's gonna bust my balls, isn't he?" He looked at the team, trying to size them up in their Royal Robbins pants, golf shirts and hockey puck watches.

Go ahead, Darwin thought. See if we fool you. He was Army for twelve years, Ranger for five of those and Delta for four, finally having to choose between retirement and a non-operational job because of his knees.

Gabe was almost 40, a cop in Detroit for fifteen years before turning to security contracting because, as he said, "It's safer." He still had the cop look, clean-shaven and professional, though every few months he'd go crazy and let a goatee hang around.

Cal Wafer was 31, a SEAL for ten years, a Team Six sniper for three of them before he moved to the private sector and really let his hair and beard grow out. He stood there in his Maui Jim sunglasses with a crooked grin on his face and let Marty cock an eyebrow at him.

Cal said, "You know where I can get a cowboy hat like that one there?"

"Just about any gas station in town," Marty said. To Darwin: "We're going to need more guns."

"This is Texas," Darwin said. "Don't they come free with the hats?"

"Oh good," Marty said. "Do the jokes cost extra? Let me break it down for you: Everybody around here is trying to kidnap or kill me."

CHAPTER 2

THEY LOADED THE gear in the back of the Suburban. Darwin kept the lockbox with him and got in the middle seat on the driver's side, Marty next to him. He'd normally be in the passenger seat, where Cal was, but this trip was about getting details. Gabe drove and Dave had the back bench to himself, sitting at an angle so he could hook one knee over the other.

They pulled into traffic, Darwin hoping Gabe remembered how to drive like a normal person after three months in Baghdad. He looked out the tinted windows at the people on the sidewalk. "So why do these folks want to kill you?"

"Not *here*, I'm talking on the job site. Out in butt-fuck Egypt. It's like the wild west out there."

"Do you know any of the threats personally?"

"Yeah, his name's Kevin."

Darwin got his notepad out, got it halfway written before Marty nudged him, smearing the ink, saying, "Hey, I'm fucking with you. Course I don't know any of them. Dave, you imagine a name like Kevin for any of those banditos?"

"Doubtful," Dave said.

Darwin closed the notepad. "Why are you a target?"

"Didn't Hank tell you all of this?"

"He did, but I want your version."

Marty sat back, started ticking his fingers. "Okay, well, we got the Juárez drug runners moving shit back and forth across the border. We got the coyotes who make a living moving illegals across. And we got the *bajadores*, the crews who run around ripping off the first two groups. Now what do all these nice folks need in order to stay in business?"

"The border," Darwin said.

"Bingo. And here I come to put up a big fuck-you surveillance tower."

"That matches my notes. Wait, I have 'fuck-off' tower."

"You know, I like that better," Marty said. He was loosening up a bit, showing off.

Sand had fallen out of Darwin's pages onto the leather seat. He tried to wipe it up.

"Leave it," Marty said. "Kind of a pisser though, huh? You leave one sandy shithole for another. Wait, let me see that."

Darwin dumped the sand into Marty's palm, thinking the guy's hand was too pink for someone that old. Marty peered at the grains, lifted his glasses, dropped them down, pushed the grains around. "It's different than here. Powdery."

"Gets into everything," Darwin said.

"I was talking to a Homeland guy yesterday, he says to me, even the Mexican sand is trying to sneak across the border. He says, it's trying to come over and steal jobs from American sand."

Darwin smiled and looked out the window, feeling Marty staring at him to get his reaction, waiting. Keep quiet, Darwin thought. Start some kind of smartass rapport with him on the first day, he'll be winking and elbowing you the whole goddam contract.

Marty looked to the back seat. "You hear him say that, Dave?"

"I wasn't there."

"Dave doesn't like to mingle. Wait, the Homeland guy

called it *wetback* sand, not Mexican sand." Marty reached into the front seat and touched Gabe on the shoulder. "Hey, no offense."

"I'm half Hawaiian," Gabe said.

Marty looked to Darwin for help.

Darwin shrugged. "He is."

Marty dumped the sand onto the floor, wiped his hand on his slacks, smacked his lips. "I'm thirsty."

Darwin heard Dave moving behind him, plastic sounds, then Dave reached over the seat with a damp bottle of water. Marty looked at the bottle, said, "I guess." He pulled the white nozzle open and squeezed water into his mouth, letting it hit the back of his throat. It made Darwin think of getting his teeth cleaned.

He said, "How safe is your work site? Well, wait. Let me start with how safe El Paso is for you."

"I'm fine here," Marty said. "When you look out the window and see the surface of the moon, we're still about two hours from the job site, but that's when my butt starts to pucker, you know? Once we're on site, I don't know. My workers are tough guys, but they're unarmed. We're just a bunch of trailers sitting there in Indian country."

"How many workers?"

"Four engineers and us."

"Spread out?" Darwin asked.

"Depends on the day. Sometimes everybody's in the same two square feet, sometimes maybe a mile or two apart for surveying. You're looking at each other. What?"

"We might need more guys," Darwin said.

"Whoa, what's that gonna cost?"

"Whatever it costs," Darwin said.

"I'm on a limited budget until this project gets officially approved."

"With Homeland money?"

"Hey," Marty said, "this isn't Iraq. People check the books around here."

"We'll see how it looks."

"We got it covered, Sheepdog," Cal said. He had his boots on the dashboard, head back, sunglasses scanning out the window. Gabe's eyes flicked front, sides, mirrors. They hit a red light and Darwin watched Gabe's neck go tight, waiting for something to happen.

Marty said, "What'd he call you? Sheepdog?"

"My call sign." Darwin said, hating this part.

"Shit, like a codename?"

"Kind of." Marty was quiet for a few beats, and when Darwin heard him take a breath he thought, Here it comes.

"What's my call sign?"

Cal turned his head just enough so Darwin could see his grin hiding in that beard. Cal nudged Gabe and kept his ear pointed at the back seat.

Darwin said, "It's pretty much just for people who'll be on the radio, so you might be okay for now."

"Oh, we have enough radios for everybody," Marty said. "I'll have to come up with something good. Dave, what's a good call sign for me?"

Fucking great, Darwin thought.

●●●

They were almost out of the sprawl around El Paso, heading southeast on 10. Darwin was curious about the landscape out the passenger side. Step across the border into Juárez, you'd better lock and load. Like rolling out of the Green Zone, but without the blast walls.

Four days earlier, Hank, the Phalanx operations manager, had stuck his head in Darwin's truck window right before they did another run along Route Irish, from the Green Zone to BIAP, the Baghdad airport.

"Hey, you and your guys wanna quick job when you rotate home day after tomorrow?"

"How quick?" Darwin said.

"Go to Texas, stay on the clock for another week or two, then home?"

"Texas? Who needs us in Texas?"

"Guy named Martin Lindy, from Lindy Survey and Construction."

Darwin looked around at the concrete walls and nests of concertina wire. "Wait, the same Lindy who put all this shit up?"

"Company's owned by his dad, but yeah, Marty helped close the deal over here."

"And now he's in Texas." Darwin turned. Cal was in the rear-facing seat, eating a banana with a belt-fed PMK between his feet. "Cal, you hear that?"

"Same rate?"

"Same," Hank said. "It's a Homeland Security project, part of the Secure Border Initiative contracted out to Boeing, who subbed this part out to Lindy. But the moolah comes from Homeland."

Cal held his banana up, twirled it in a circle: Good to go. Darwin checked Gabe. He was rubbing the back of his neck. "What is it?" he asked.

Hank said, "Personal protection on Lindy, static on the job site. Just follow him around, make sure nobody grabs him or blows his toys up."

"In Texas," Darwin said.

"On the border, near Juárez. I'll put something together for the flight, get your Texas creds ready."

"Are we crossing the border?"

"Not that I know of, but you'll have your passports."

Darwin said, "I was thinking more about weapons permits."

Hank leaned in the window, made sure Cal could hear him. "If you cross into Mexico with firearms, you will be considered a hostile invading army. I'll probably be able to get you out of prison in sixty years."

Darwin looked over again. "Gabe, your vote?"

"Do I have to listen to country music?"

"I don't have that information," Hank said.

"Eh. I'll risk it."

Darwin said, "Who else?"

"For now, just you guys," Hank said. "I have a bigger team available in two weeks, Warner and his guys, but everybody's tied up 'til then."

Darwin chewed his gum and looked through the windshield. Hank raised his eyebrows and tried a thumbs-up. Darwin said, "Okay. But you gotta call my wife and tell her."

"Hey, fuck you. Get out of the truck, I'd rather get blown up."

CHAPTER 3

THE RIDE OUT of El Paso was quiet for a while, Darwin watching the landscape turn into something very close to the low hills in Afghanistan when Marty said, "Hey, who would you guys rather shoot, a terrorist or a drug dealer?"

Gabe and Cal looked at each other. Gabe shook his head once, went back to driving, but Cal looked like he was thinking it over.

Darwin said, "From what I gather, the drug dealers around here *are* terrorists. Kidnappings, executions, ambushing cops."

"More than that," Marty said. "Out in the hills where we are, the cartels hire former Mexican army commandos as enforcers. They roam back and forth across the border, pretty much do whatever they want."

Cal said, "Mexican commandos? Uh oh."

Darwin liked to think of his team as three circles on a piece of paper, each one with a set of skills that complemented the other two. Put the three circles in a triangle with a little overlap in the middle, and that's where the principle went, cozy and safe. And usually bitching about something.

Or worse: Marty was the kind of principle who liked to walk around, show off his protection. Tell him he shouldn't go somewhere, lots of people there who want to shoot him, he'll say, "Yeah? We'll show them."

●●●

Three hours later they stopped in Marfa and got some food, Darwin's jet lag telling him it wasn't dinner time, what's with the burger? Gabe said he was fine driving, wouldn't relax anyway if he was a passenger, so they got in the same seats and headed southwest on 67, the land spreading away from them in low brown hills and scrub brush. Ten minutes out Marty was sleeping, wedged into the corner of the seat and door, muttering about something. Guy doesn't even shut up in his sleep, Darwin thought.

He pulled the stack of files Marty had given him onto his lap, details on the kind of work Lindy Construction was doing here. There were a lot of references to core samples and bedrock fissures. He fanned the pages again, looking for pictures. There still weren't any. Fourteen hours on a plane, most of it asleep, and this shit was closing his eyes.

They topped a rise and got the setting sun full in the windshield and Darwin thought Cal was kidding when he said, "Contact right."

Darwin looked up grinning, expecting a jackrabbit or a man-shaped cactus, but it was a Jeep coming from the desert at their one o'clock, fast, the sun behind it. Gabe accelerated, pushed the Suburban over 80 and kept his foot down. Darwin reached across his lap for the M4, found the pile of papers.

"Shit." He went to his thigh for the .45, looked at the lockbox on the floor next to his feet. "Goddamit."

Cal said, "What are we, on fucking vacation?"

"Hold on," Darwin said. Stupid, stupid. He dumped the

papers and looked over the back of his seat. "Dave, lie down on the bench there." He pulled the lockbox up into his lap, hitting Marty's leg on the way by, Marty snorting and looking around.

"S'fast," he said, watching the landscape fly.

Darwin had the box open. "Marty, keep your head down. Get down in the footwell."

"What?"

Darwin put his Springfield .45 1911 to the side, handed Cal's Sig Sauer P226 9mm forward, then Gabe's Glock 9mm and spare magazines for both. Cal checked the inserted mags, worked the slides to go hot and put the guns on Safe. "How many inside?"

"Can't tell yet," Gabe said. He stuck the Glock in the console cup holder.

Cal got his window down and held the Sig below the sill with his left hand. He was right-handed but it didn't matter. "Guess we shoulda put our helmets in carry-on."

Darwin got a live round in the .45 and put two spare mags in the pocket on the back of Gabe's seat. "Marty, down."

"What's going on?" Marty looked into the back seat. "What happened to *Dave?*"

"I'm following orders," Dave said from the floor.

Darwin reached over and got a handful of Marty's collar, shoved him down into the footwell behind Cal. "Stay there."

The three of them watched the Jeep. It kept on the same line, faster now, even twitched left and right to keep an intercepting angle.

"Border Patrol?" Darwin said.

The sun was too much for Cal's sunglasses. He blocked it with a hand. "I don't see any markings. Do they know we're around?"

"Hank was supposed to file the paperwork. Marty, did you talk to the Border Patrol?"

Marty had his fingers in his ears.

Cal said, "I get killed because Hank was downloading

porn, I'm gonna be pissed."

Gabe rode the centerline, no traffic in sight, giving himself room on each side of the Suburban. The Jeep was a half mile out, kicking up a dust cloud that could hide a convoy. Darwin checked the angles; the Jeep was going to cut them off.

"It's tan," Gabe said. "The Jeep is tan."

Darwin reached down and pulled on Marty's arm. "You have any workers out here? Any tan Jeeps?"

Marty was shaking, his knees pulled up to his chin. He kept tilting his head and looking at the window above him like a dinosaur was going to come through it and eat him up.

"Marty," Darwin said.

"Ah, at the site, yes. Our crew is there. Not out here."

Darwin had to be sure. "Dave?"

"No Jeeps," Dave said from the floor.

Darwin leaned between the front seats. "Border has white trucks, white and green. If it's Border, we have to stop."

"I know," Gabe said.

They weren't used to it. Rolling in Iraq, they didn't stop for anybody except Big Army and another contractor. Well, he thought, most contractors. But stop for the Iraqi police, you're likely to get shoved in a trunk with a bag over your head.

A quarter mile ahead, the Jeep swerved to hit the highway at a 90-degree angle and block them.

"I see two pax," Cal said, "driver and passenger. They're checking us. Now they're waving."

"Fuck 'em," Darwin said.

"We got loose sand on the left side," said Gabe.

The Jeep pulled across the road and stopped a few hundred yards ahead. Gabe slid into the oncoming lane and sped up. The Jeep rolled forward, its front tires on the sand to block that lane and push the Suburban into the desert.

"Hold on," Darwin told everybody.

Gabe cut right, the Suburban rocking on its suspension

and almost tilting onto two tires, roaring toward the Jeep's back bumper. Darwin could see the driver watching them, a young Mexican guy, seeing they weren't going to stop, saying something, his teeth showing as he gunned it off the road to get out of the way.

Darwin twisted in his seat, saw the Jeep curl after them and accelerate, sliding around until it got back on the pavement, then moving fast. Catching up.

"Nitrous," Cal said, staring at his mirror. "That thing's built for moving shit across the desert."

"We're not gonna outrun them," Gabe said. He patted the dashboard, letting the Suburban know it wasn't her fault.

Darwin thought about it, said, "Three of us, two of them. Screw it, slow down. Let's see what they have to say."

Gabe pulled into the right lane and eased off the gas. The Jeep was already drifting left to come up alongside.

Cal turned in his seat to face out the driver's side. "If this is a snatch job, it's piss-poor. No blocking vehicle, no chase car. These jackasses have to do it all themselves."

"Sounds like us," Darwin said. "Marty, stay down."

"Oh God."

"You're okay. Dave, you good?"

"Yes."

"Call somebody," Marty said. "Call 911."

Cal laughed. "911, is this an emergency? Yeah, we're about to shoot it out with some assholes. Can you bring more ammo?"

●●●

The Jeep rolled up next to them, both vehicles going about fifty-five now. The driver kept his eyes on the road but the passenger was staring at Darwin's window, not crazy or pissed, almost confused. The guy looked in his 40s, short salt and pepper hair and stubble, Latino for sure, but Darwin didn't think he was Mexican.

"Giving you the stink eye," Cal said.

"He's staring at his reflection," Darwin said. "These windows are dark as hell. You see any weapons?"

"Nope."

"Gabe?"

Gabe glanced over. "Just the whole Jeep, he decides to ram us."

The guy brought his hand up and Darwin almost fired through the glass but the guy just cranked his fist around, wanting Darwin to roll his window down.

"What the fuck?" Darwin said. "Marty, you know this guy?"

Marty had assumed the crash position and wasn't budging.

Darwin said, "What do you guys think?"

"Maybe he's lost," Cal said.

Gabe got the Glock in his right hand, below the sill. "Go ahead."

Darwin had the .45's barrel almost touching the base of his window, the skateboard tape around the grip married to his palm. He hit the switch and put the glass halfway down, the guy relaxing when it started to move but right back to confused when he saw Darwin looking back at him.

They stared. The Jeep's knobby tires attacked the pavement.

The guy said, "Who are you?"

"What do you want?" Darwin said back.

The guy was about to say something, got a look on his face like it was a trap and shut his mouth. Then: "Where did you get this truck?"

His English was perfect, a little accent Darwin couldn't place. "That's not what you were gonna say."

"So?"

"Whose truck did you think this was?"

The guy stared at him, a smile pulling at one side. He made a gun with his finger and thumb, pointed it at Darwin. "How about you pull over?"

Darwin rolled his window all the way down, showed him the front sight and manhole barrel of the .45. Gabe's window was dropping, his Glock riding the top of the glass down. Cal leaned across the driver's seat to get his Sig through the opening, steady on the driver.

Darwin said, "How about you fuck off down the road?" He was nice about it, but serious.

The guy took it all in, looked at the finger gun and pretended to drop it out of the Jeep. He put his hands up and said something to the driver, who finally looked over and saw the guns. He pulled straight back on the steering wheel so hard he lifted himself out of his seat.

Darwin thought: That guy might be shitting himself.

The passenger said to Darwin, "I'll see you." He nodded to the driver, who half relaxed and hit a switch on the dash. The Jeep's engine climbed to a new frequency and the thing was gone, cutting in front of them and angling into the desert, dust trail folding over in the breeze.

"Clear," Darwin said. Cal and Gabe responded with the same, all three of them clicking to Safe. Darwin looked down at Marty, holding his water bottle to his cheek and trying to control his breathing.

"Well Marty," Darwin said, "you're right. We're gonna need more guns."

CHAPTER 4

MARO BOUNCED AROUND in the Jeep's passenger seat, the driver still scared of the funny shooters. That was funny too, but he was going to roll the Jeep. Maro couldn't see the road anymore, too many hills between them now, but he could feel them back there. Laughing, probably.

"Slow down," he told the driver. Maro knew he didn't like taking orders from a Cuban, but too fucking bad. The kid with peach fuzz for a mustache slowed down.

A bit.

"Stop," Maro finally said.

The kid stopped, said, "I didn't know what to do. I'm sorry."

"You're fine," Maro told him. He got out of the Jeep and looked southeast, toward the Lindy construction site. He couldn't think in the Jeep. In Afghanistan, when the Russians had brought him in to fight the guerrillas for his twentieth birthday, Jeeps were rolling coffins. Anything with wheels or tracks, don't wear your nice clothes. Leave them for someone who's still in one piece. He needed the sand under his feet, the rocks and plants pulling him along, showing him, look: A track.

They were here.

They went this way.

Let's get them.

He walked southwest, toward the border, trying to figure it out. The Jeep idled along next to him, the kid glancing over to make sure he was driving okay.

Maro tugged out his *saperka*, the Russian entrenching tool that hung down behind his right leg, and the kid made a noise in his throat. Maro waved him down, showing him look, I just want to swing it around, feel the weight of it while I think. The Spetznaz in Afghanistan had given it to him, shown him how to use it close up and throw it, better than a knife in hand-to-hand combat. For taking people apart, heads off necks, it was hard work but worth the effect.

He gave it a lazy swing, thinking what to do about what just happened. Walk into the construction site, ask everybody: What the hell was that all about?

They wouldn't expect that.

No, better: Go at night, find the man from the back seat, with the .45. Tap him on the chest with the shovel and wake him up. Tell him: I fucked off down the road, now what?

Maro smiled about it, knowing that would be a bad idea. Staring at the guy back on the road, they'd recognized each other.

Not as acquaintances, but as men who knew how to do things.

Like fighters at a weigh-in, seeing your opponent's eyes up close for the first time. Seeing what he had in him.

Maro stopped walking.

The Jeep stopped next to him.

"Tell the rest of the men," Maro said, "from now on, automatic weapons at all times. Both sides of the border. Okay?"

"Okay, yes."

"Good boy." He started walking again, feeling the sand beneath him, thinking: Who will throw the first punch?

CHAPTER 5

DARWIN STOOD WITH Cal and Gabe at the back of the Suburban, the sun just touching the horizon. They looked around at the construction site and did a short hot wash, breaking down what happened on the road and what to do next.

The site was smack in the middle of nowhere, less than a mile from the Rio Grande and Mexico, twenty miles away from the nearest US town, five hours if you stuck to the roads. The Rio went almost north to south here and it felt weird to Darwin, having the border to the west like that. He liked to think of the sun setting off California's coast, not behind hills in Mexico.

The land sloped downhill to the river, sparse vegetation and rocky dirt until it got close to the water and the brush got thick, like a hedgerow. On the other side the heavy brush continued up the hillsides, some big rocks and game trails breaking it up until the rock face got too steep and only a few plants could hold on.

There were three white job trailers lined up and sitting on chunks of wood and cinderblocks, then a red Conex shipping container, forty feet long, eight wide, eight and a half high, the double doors closed. Two Toyota pickups were parked in the long shade of the container. Darwin could hear the drone of a generator running somewhere nearby, and there was a flat, square area of dirt and gravel a couple hundred yards to the southwest that had to be where the tower was going up. It was a few hundred feet on each side, about half the size of a football field, with a blue Conex box at the edge of the gravel.

A few tan guys in jeans and Lindy golf shirts were wandering around the place, trying to look like they weren't checking out the new arrivals.

Cal took it all in. "How'd they get this shit back in here?"

"Slowly," Gabe said.

They'd gone about thirty miles after the point of contact, then turned onto a two-track for another slow fifteen, everybody waiting for another hit that didn't come. Marty was a mess, heading straight to the trailer on the far left, Dave helping him up the wooden stairs.

Darwin appreciated that his guys acted like it was just another day, and hey, it was. They'd taken the adrenaline dump, stayed calm, and got through it. Now he wanted some Pepsi, something to level them off and help the crash.

"You get a good look at the passenger?" he asked.

"Dude was hard," Cal said. "Ain't the first time he's had guns in his face."

Gabe nodded. "Agreed. The driver was amateur hour, but our boy's been there, done that."

Darwin said, "So which one is he: drugs, coyote, or the rip-off guys? What the hell was it—the *bajadores*."

"That'd be good to know," Cal said.

They all thought about it, trying to find an angle to the answer. Darwin let it go after a few seconds; if it wasn't there yet, no point waiting for it.

He said, "You know, I'm kinda glad that happened right away. I got off the plane feeling like I was on vacation, nobody giving us the evil eye. I looked at people talking on cell phones and told myself: Relax, they aren't triggering an IED. We get out here and nothing happens for four days, then we get hit, man. I don't know if I'd be ready."

"For these clowns?" Cal said, his thumb jacked toward the border.

"See, that's what I mean. We think like that, let our guard down, somebody's getting hurt."

Gabe said, "I hear you, but it does feel good to walk around without thinking about mortars dropping in or the guy next to you blowing himself up."

Darwin nodded. "All I'm saying, let's treat this job like what it is. We're on home field and nobody has a jihad out on us, but we saw today there's still a risk."

"But this is so relaxing," Gabe said, presenting the horizon. "Right now we have a full three hundred and sixty degrees of exposure and potential entry points."

They ran through an actions-on list, all the 'What if?' scenarios and 'What then?' follow-ups they could think of. The brief rehearsals confirmed it: the location was a nightmare.

"River's key," Cal said. "We need to find out if there's a crossing nearby, which way shooters will come from if they come. Hey, see if we can tell where our buddy in the Jeep went, if he crossed over."

Darwin thought about the guy again, the way he'd reacted when the back window went down. "He was genuinely surprised to see us in that truck. We gotta find out how common dark blue Suburbans are around here."

Gabe said, "I can ask around tomorrow when I go in for the long guns."

"Both of you go. Nobody rides alone."

"Leaves you solo," Cal said.

Darwin looked around. "Any unfriendlies show up, I'll lock everybody in a Conex, set some fires, strip naked and run around screaming."

"That old trick," Cal said. "Hey, that reminds me, you call your wife yet?"

"Ah fuck."

●●●

Darwin stepped away from the Suburban, gave the finger over his shoulder to Cal and Gabe grinning and whispering to each other. He found some high ground, just a little bump on the easy slope down to the Rio, but it made him feel good, gave him a view. The colors had changed in the sunset, everything looking a little burnt or rusty, and nothing was moving except the guys behind him.

He checked his phone: Full signal.

Damn.

Just get it over with.

He scrolled through the recent calls, all the way to the bottom, and she wasn't on the list. Well, that tells you something right there, huh? Found her in the Contacts, got the call going. It rang at the other end and he willed it to go to voicemail.

"You know what time it is here?" she said.

Every time.

"Yeah, two hours later than it is here."

That made her think. "Wait, what? Where are you?"

"Texas."

"*Texas*? Are you messing with me?"

"Nope. I can't say exactly where, but I am indeed in Texas."

"What the hell for?"

"Work, Christine."

"Work. For how long? You're supposed to be home tomorrow."

Darwin knelt down, his knees popping like champagne corks, and tossed a rock to see how far it would roll. Not far enough. "A week or two. We don't know for sure yet."

Silence. Not good.

"Well, that's just great," she said.

"I'm sorry, Hank needed a team."

"Who gives a shit what Hank needs?"

"Christine," he said. He couldn't remember the last time he'd called her Baby, Sweetie.

"Which way did you go?" she asked.

"Which way?"

"New York? DC?"

"We flew into Miami, caught another to Texas."

"Oh," she said. "You better not have been up here and not stopped by."

"What, just land the jet on I-94, tell 'em hold on a sec?"

She was quiet for a bit and Darwin thought he'd gone too far. She said, "Well, I'm horny. And you need to sign the divorce papers."

"Christine."

"Patrick."

"Will you tear that up like I asked?"

"It was *your* idea."

"No, no," he said, "you told me you were going to get the papers, and I said go ahead."

"See?"

"I was bluffing," Darwin said.

"I wasn't. They're right here on the kitchen counter."

He stood up, squinted at the sun cut in half by the hills to the west. He could feel the ground giving up its heat already. "Christine, just wait, okay? We'll figure it out."

"I already figured it out: You don't *want* to figure it out. You just wanna keep putting it off while you go play guns. That's why I got the papers. Now hurry up and get here, because I need it bad and I'm not gonna cheat on you."

"That's nice."

Her voice dropped. "Don't you want it?"

"Goddammit, Christine, don't start. I'm out here in the fucking desert."

She giggled. "You can sign the papers on my back."

"I'll call you when I know more."

"It better be soon."

"Okay. Be safe."

"Yeah, you too."

He waited to see if she'd say it. He'd say it back.

"Bye," she said, and hung up.

He checked the sun again, dropping fast, then headed back to the trailers, adjusting the front of his pants.

"How'd it go?" Cal asked, his whole beard smiling.

Darwin said, "Somebody please fucking shoot me."

●●●

The trailer on the left was Marty's office, the door halfway down the side that faced away from the other trailers, a big desk and chair on the right as Darwin and his guys stepped in. There was a meeting table in the middle with folding chairs around it, white boards on the far wall with sketches and science drawn all over, names and phone numbers and a quote, "What would MacGuyver do?"

Dave was sitting on a low couch to the left of the door, legs crossed and lips pursed. He looked at the handguns strapped to their legs, kept his eyes down there and said, "Marty's lying down." He tilted his head toward the wall that closed off the last third of the trailer, wood paneling with double pocket doors set in the middle. In the far corner there was a tall wire bin with rolled-up blueprints standing up in it.

"How you doing?" Darwin said. He and Cal and Gabe found chairs and faced the couch and Marty's door.

"Not bad. Still a little shaky. That was a . . . new experience."

Darwin pointed at him. "You did great. Stayed calm, did like I asked. Well, *told*, but I appreciate it."

Dave waved him off. Cal had his sunglasses pushed up on his head, holding his hair out of his face. He looked like he was there for a meeting about welding or the drywall.

He said, "How's Mr. Marty holding up?"

Dave looked at the door, listened for movement, kept his voice low. "I think he was sick, when we got back. I could hear it. He had a few drinks and said to wake him up before you guys came in."

"Whoops," Gabe said.

"You mind stepping out and I'll get him up and around?"

Darwin had his legs straight out, stretching his knees, and wanted a way to stand up without bending them. He gave up and was about to stand when the pocket doors slid open, Marty standing there with his hair angling off. He had his glasses in his hand and squinted in the light at everybody, put the glasses on and blinked.

He sniffed and shot Dave a look.

"They just came in," Dave said.

Marty ignored him. The space behind Marty had a small kitchen and bar, then a short hallway with a half-open bathroom door. The hallway led to a bedroom, and in the dim indirect lighting Darwin could see the blankets all messed up.

Marty lifted a squat glass off the counter. It had amber liquid at the bottom and water and half-melted ice cubes at the top. He swirled it around, got it mixed, took a sip, smacked his lips. "You guys want a drink?"

"Pepsi if you got it, water if not," Darwin said.

Dave stood up, Marty waved him back down. "I got it." He reached into a mini fridge by his leg and pulled three cans of Pepsi, set them on the table in front of Gabe. "What time is it?"

"Nine forty," Dave said.

"Jesus, feels like midnight. What do you guys think of the place?" Marty squeezed past them and sat at his desk, making them all turn so they could see him. Dave stayed where he was, out of it now.

"Good sight lines," Darwin said, "but that works both ways."

"Meaning?"

"Meaning if somebody wants to shoot you instead of snatch you, he can do it from a long way out."

"Ah." Marty took another sip.

"How hard is it to move these trailers around?"

"To where?"

"I'd like to get a triangle going," Darwin said, "a protected middle for people moving from trailer to trailer."

"That's probably not going to happen," Marty said. "It's a lot of work getting the foundations stable, level, set just right. And we'd have to get the hauler back out here, or something with forks on it. I can see about it when we relocate to the next tower site."

"When is that?"

Marty swiveled in his chair, back and forth. "Two months, give or take."

Darwin turned to Cal. "How far does a bullet go in two months?"

"Which kind?"

"All right," Marty said, "I get it. Is it life or death?"

"It would be better," Darwin said, "but if a guy wants to snipe you out here, he'll get his chance."

"So it's not worth the hassle."

"You have body armor?"

Marty squinted at him, like it was a trick. "No."

"We have extra, but not enough for everybody. Order some for you and all your guys, level three. Gabe can show you some websites. They can wear it under their shirts."

"How hot is it?" Marty asked.

Darwin tapped the table, took a breath. "It's hot. They'll get used to it."

Marty finished his drink, the ice hitting him in the nose. He set the glass down and didn't wipe his face, just stared off.

"Look," Darwin said, "this stays in the trailer for now, but the way we see it, it's your men in danger of getting killed, not you."

Marty frowned.

"To the guys who profit off the border, you're worth more alive than dead. They want ransoms. I'm sure they don't like the tower you're trying to build, but they gotta know, they kill you today, the next lowest bidder will be here tomorrow."

"We weren't the lowest bidder," Marty said.

"Nevertheless," Darwin said. "If they're smart, they'll kill the workers. Shoot 'em, snatch 'em and leave body parts around, blow 'em up. Pretty soon nobody will work for you or anybody else building the tower."

"I don't know about that," Marty said. "Our bennies are pretty good."

"You cover funerals? Let me finish. The whole kill the workers plan will eventually backfire, because DC will drop the hammer and get the National Guard here to put the tower up. Then everybody's fucked. But in the meantime, they delay the tower and maybe get some nice payoffs if they can grab you and anybody else worth keeping alive."

Darwin turned.

"Dave, you keep wearing that suit. It might be better than body armor, far as getting shot at goes."

Dave smoothed his tie. "Right."

The room was quiet for a few beats until Cal cleared his throat. "You have anything you can set up around this place? Like a construction fence?"

Marty said, "I think we have some in the shippers. I can get on the radio, get Jim to check. You can meet him and the other guys." Marty stood and leaned over his desk to look out a window that faced the middle trailer. "Lights are out, they might be cashed."

"Let's save it for tomorrow," Darwin said.

Cal said, "You got any razor wire?"

Marty froze halfway down to his chair, looked from Cal

to Darwin. "He's serious?"

"Have you seen his beard?"

●●●

They cracked the Pepsis and Gabe looked at the whiteboard, said, "So what is this, some kind of gun tower?"

"I wish," Marty said. "Helluva lot easier to build one of those. Okay, so we got the Secure Border Initiative, and this is SBI*net*, pretty much a virtual fence, a bunch of tower stations and command centers, all hooked up to aerial surveillance and Border Patrol. Plus some real fences and roads, vehicle barriers, but we're still working on getting that contract. A while back they drove a bunch of mobile towers around to find the best spots, and now we come in and build a permanent one. Then we move on to the next spot they picked and start all over."

"Sounds like how Terminator got started," Cal said.

Marty pointed at him. "You're not far off. Most people this side of the border like it, say it's better than a big wall messing with the animals and landscape. But on the other side, across the Rio? Even the law abiders are pissed about it."

"Offended?" Darwin said.

"That, and picture a big ass highway, like eight lanes. You put a blockade in the middle lane, then the lanes next to it, what happens?"

Cal said, "All these criminals are gonna flow around the ends of the fence."

"Bingo. Some of these Mexican towns have, like one murder every five years, because some asshole stole another guy's *burro*, and now they got scumbags cutting off heads and leaving them in suitcases around town. They can't handle it."

Darwin said, "Why don't you start at the ends, funnel

everything into the middle? Park a few tanks there and see what happens."

"You know, I been taking calls from a lady with Border Patrol, works out of Big Bend to the south, and she says the same thing. She knows the sheriffs across the river, says they're gonna get the worst of it when these towers get going. And this chick, Christ, you see her walking down the street, in that uniform? I'm guilty, take me in."

Darwin said, "So if everybody knows there's a better way…"

"I thought you worked for the government. But hey, we might end up doing that. The start at the ends part, not the tanks, though I wish to hell we could. But when you start out, just have this one station going up, you know? It's both ends *and* the middle."

Cal leaned back, put his boots on the table. "It's a big-ass target is what it is."

CHAPTER 6

MARO WATCHED THE trailers from a half mile away, the Rio behind him and his worn AK-47 next to him on a patch of scrub grass. Not much had happened once the sun went down, the big light hanging off the red container giving the whole scene an alien look, but he stayed and listened to the night animals moving around him and watched.

He was alone but could get on his phone and bring in his killers if he needed them. They were across the river and on the other side of the ridge, tucked into the shallow caves with all the daytime workers. The night shift was probably starting now. Maro had looked for any way to speed it up, get the project done faster, but the work was hard. And dangerous, sure.

Around ten o'clock the trailer on the left opened and three men came out, the first one stocky and maybe Mexican, the driver from earlier. The second one, from the passenger seat, was white but tan and tall with an amazing beard. The third was the man Maro had spoken with on the road. He stood in the doorway, talking to someone inside, then closed the door and walked down the steps shaking his head and smiling.

He said something to the other two and they laughed, all of them turning when the trailer door opened and Martin

Lindy stuck his head out, his hair a mess. He looked at his watch and told the three men something then shut the door.

Maro watched the three men move toward the trailer on the right. They talked, pointed out at the landscape, seemed at one time to stare right at him but he knew better.

He thought for a few seconds about getting closer, putting all three of them down on their first day here. He worked how he would do it and get away safely, but it was just for fun. One thing the cartel didn't always understand: You shoot one American, *all* of them shoot back.

That was one of the reasons they brought him in. He could be smart about things and not worry about ego and status. They let him pick his killers and bring in a few of his own officers to keep the locals under control. It was interesting, putting soldiers in charge of flat-out murderers, savages. He'd seen it before, and it almost always pulled the soldiers down into the butchery instead of going the other way. His officers were telling him: These boys are used to killing people often, and they miss it.

Maro watched the three men and thought about how he'd have to give his guys someone to kill soon, or they'd get bored and wander off, maybe try to kill Maro first.

That would be too bad. He liked his *salvajes*, his savages, and hoped he wouldn't have to kill them all. They called his AK *cuerno de chivo*, goat's horn, and he liked that.

He watched the three men walk up the steps to the trailer on the right and go inside, lights coming on in there. He stood up, stretched, and picked up his rifle. He moved forward with soft feet, angled so he could loop around and get to the trailer on the left without being seen.

●●●

Darwin moved through the third trailer, one big room with a bathroom at the left end, and found the cots collapsed and stacked up in the corner. The trailer looked like it was for worker overflow and storage, dust on the inside of the windows and a card table with folding lawn chairs set up inside the door. The low carpet had coffee and oil stains and lighter shapes with corners where furniture had sat for years. He pulled one cot off the stack.

"Where's the snoring area?"

"You want me to sleep outside?" Cal said. He set two of their bags, mostly clothes and laptops, down on the card table.

"Just wait," Gabe said, "you're gonna drop off and start your buzzsaw, and Marty's guys are gonna come running, thinking the generator's falling apart."

Darwin opened the cot, shoved the head against the wall. "What gets me is he can turn it on and off. We go to the border and set up a listening post, he'll be a field mouse."

"Can't you just pretend you're on a watch?" Gabe asked Cal.

"Can't you just pretend you're deaf?"

"Huh?"

Darwin got the second cot going. "I suppose we should set up a night watch."

Cal said, "It'd be fucking embarrassing to get killed by a Mexican commando in my sleep."

Darwin nodded. "I keep picturing Pancho Villa wearing all black, a big ol' mustachio sticking out of a balaclava."

"That's racist," Cal said.

Darwin straightened up, thought about it. "I guess it is."

"Racism earns first watch," Gabe said.

"I'm cured." Darwin looked at the lawn chairs, all straps and aluminum tubing. Nothing soft. "I need a footstool."

Gabe had his laptop open on the card table, checking the satellite broadband connection. "I didn't like those hills to the southwest. Those were across the Rio, right?"

"Gotta be," Darwin said.

"Good place for a dude with a spotting scope to keep track of us."

Cal said, "Have to get closer to plink anybody, unless they got themselves a world-class shooter."

"Not impossible," Darwin said.

"Tell you what, we all start saluting Marty out in the open, we'll find out real quick if they got a shooter who respects the chain of command."

Darwin said, "Guys, don't sniper check the client." The cots had thin mattresses with stains he didn't want to identify. "How we looking on the crates?"

Gabe already had the site up. "Tracking has it coming in on a cargo plane, 5 a.m. We'll go first thing."

Darwin said, "I'll get the Suburban keys. Let Marty know it'll be just me and him for mimosas."

Cal leaned on the table, said to Gabe, just loud enough: "Let's hit that IHOP we saw on the way out of El Paso."

Darwin ignored them, pulled on his 5.11 Sabre jacket, Coyote Brown, good for this landscape. He clapped a lawn chair flat and grabbed a flashlight out of the gear bag, a radio, found his Karambit folding knife and clipped it to his pocket. Heading out the door he stopped, looked at both of them.

"If you don't bring me pancakes, I'll feed you to the scorpions."

●●●

Maro was on a line to the trailer on the left, letting his feet find the way while he looked up at the stars. He liked them, for one thing, and the construction site had that bright white light and he didn't want it to ruin his night vision. The trailer had lights in the windows too.

The lights, to him, said: Hey, shoot this way.

He was close enough now that he couldn't see any of the other trailers, just the one he'd seen Martin Lindy poke out of. He heard a door open and close, the next trailer over or the furthest one.

He stopped and crouched next to a pile of scrub brush, waited. Brought his head down with his eyes closed, got them looking at the ground before he opened them. The barrel of the AK swept with his eyes to the corners of the trailer, left, then right as the man from the back seat walked around and leaned a lawn chair against the trailer before he walked up the stairs. Maro let the barrel drop. The man knocked once and opened the door, closed it behind him.

Maro could hear them talking in there, sounds but nothing he could pick out as words.

What now?

Shoot him when he comes out, that would get things going.

Things. What *things*? Act like a professional.

Maro shook his head. He *was* acting like a professional. Who cares if he took a few seconds to think about doing crazy things like he used to? When the Russians cut him loose in the Panjshir Valley and said, "Just let us know when you need more bullets."

He told them, "What happens when I need more targets?"

Okay, but what about this, now?

Well, you came all this way.

He went forward and kept his eyes down away from the bright windows while he ducked under the trailer stairs.

•••

Darwin stood just inside the door with the Suburban's key ring on his finger, flipping it around, and kept looking between Dave and Marty to keep them both in the conversation, telling them about the security watch and the trip in the morning.

"I may have them bring another rental truck back," he said, "so we can have a CAT following you and whoever you're riding with. Which will usually be me."

"Cat?" Dave said.

"Counter-assault team. A truckload of weapons and guys who want to use them. If there's a shark attack on the road the CAT rolls in and shoots everything so we can break contact. We're short, so Gabe and Cal may have to work that truck while I drive you."

Marty swiveled in his chair, short arcs. "We can use one of the pickups."

"Could get shot up."

He shrugged. "Isn't that true no matter what?"

"Solid logic. You guys all set for the night?"

"Soon as I kill this," Marty said, his glass halfway to his mouth, "I'm calling it a day. And hey, breakfast is in the middle trailer. It has the big kitchen and all the food."

"Good enough." Darwin popped the door open. "Sleep fast gentlemen."

He stepped out and closed the door and a switch flipped inside him. He turned, looked around. The single halogen on the Conex was on the side away from the trailer, dumping this side in shadow with a halo about twenty feet out, showing some scrub and a few prickly pears.

He felt it though. Not the itch on the back of his neck or between his shoulder blades when someone was scoping him, but close. Like someone had just called, "Rolling," and they were waiting for the action to start.

He put one hand on the wooden railing and the other on the .45 and waited.

Nothing.

He gave it a few more seconds, still felt it but thought it might be the new place, new energy he wasn't used to yet.

"Huh," he said.

He walked down the steps and grabbed the lawn chair and headed around the corner to find a vantage point, waiting to see if the feeling followed him.

●●●

Marty took the full glass from Dave and got more of the Scotch down, wishing he had some olives or pickles to snack on. He'd pay a million dollars if someone would open a 7-11 within twenty five miles.

Dave had that pursed-up look, like he had something to say but wouldn't let it out until Marty asked for it. Maybe tomorrow, he thought. If Dave couldn't sleep that was his problem. He stood there next to where Darwin had been, looking at it, then back at Marty.

Goddam it.

"What?" Marty said.

Dave sat down on the couch, his mouth open to talk when the trailer door opened. They both looked over and saw a dark, rough hand snake through the opening, pat around the wall until it found the light switch, and flick them off.

"Hey," Marty said, blinking in the darkness, his head moving around like it would help. He could hear someone step into the trailer, the door close, then nothing.

"Okay, very funny. I guess I'm, what, *vul*nerable."

Just breathing. And a new smell, what he'd call earthy.

"Dave?"

"I'm here."

"Who else?"

"I don't know." Dave cleared his throat. To the room:

"Hello?"

Marty heard, "It's me." Then a chair scraping and creaking under new weight.

"Jesus Christ, Maro?"

"Yes."

Marty held his hands palms up, realized it was still dark and nobody could see it. "Uh, the lights?"

"Let's leave them off. So anyone outside won't see us talking."

•••

Darwin found a spot uphill from the trailers, looking across them toward the Rio and the dark hills. He got the chair right and moved it until a flap of prickly pear was between his eyes and the light hanging off the Conex box. Still not ideal for his night vision, but he could see everything without having spots when he blinked.

He trusted his ears for everything behind him, but still gave it all a quick look, making sure someone wasn't already standing around back there. He kept the flashlight and radio in his lap, had the weight of the .45 on his thigh.

He saw the lights go out in Marty's trailer, waited for one to pop on in Marty's bedroom right there on the end facing Darwin, but it didn't happen.

Good thing. He didn't think there were any blinds on those windows, and he didn't want to see Marty walking around in his boxers—nah, he was a whitey tighty guy—fiddling with himself and flopping around in bed until he got comfortable.

Where the hell did Dave sleep? Darwin pictured him sitting upright on the couch, powering down like an android, his eyes popping open as soon as Marty had his first ball scratch the next morning.

Well, they were tucked in, that's all that mattered.

He stretched out, felt and heard the pressure pop out of his knees. Thought again about getting the surgery done, but the idea of all the physical therapy, the down time . . .

Not being able to run away from Christine.

He pulled his phone out, almost sent her a text. Start out nice, see if she wanted to get into something fun over the phone. His heart sped up a bit at the thought of it, his throat getting a little tight.

Goddam it.

Describe what you're doing, she'll say, "A *lawn* chair? Shouldn't you be walking around, patrolling?"

Like she knew better. Or he was cutting corners.

He put the phone away, wondering how that spell of hers worked everywhere on the planet.

●●●

Marty's eyes were adjusting. He could see the outline of Maro's head and shoulders against the window in the door. He tapped his desk, found his glass and took another drink. "I'll tell you, my heart's about had it for today."

He wanted Maro to ask him, Why is that? Tell him the story the way he wanted, Dave would stay quiet. But Maro said, "Oh, were you there on the highway today?"

"That was *you?*"

"I had something to tell you, but someone else was in your truck. I didn't see you in there."

"Yeah, bullshit." Maro didn't say anything to that and Marty finally said, "I thought it was the fucking Lunas after me. Or, shit, the Border Patrol."

"The cartel won't send anyone here while I'm working. So

I know, I see someone I don't recognize, it's okay to shoot them."

Marty said, "What about the other cartels?"

"Well, that could happen. Like I told you before though, for them to move in I must be dead already. So I won't worry about it."

Marty could picture him in the dark, that smirk like he was daring someone to push him on it. Best to let it go, let him beat his chest a little, but Marty said, "If that happens, you get killed, can you call me on my cell? So I can be ready?"

"You'll know," Maro said. "Just watch for the mushroom cloud."

●●●

Dave banged his way back from the kitchen and put the water somewhere near Maro, who said thank you and cracked the top. Marty could see just about everything now and felt relaxed in the dark. Long as he knew where Maro was, sitting in the same chair Darwin had used. Marty had heard the handle of that shovel thing he carried knock against the chair's frame.

Marty said, "So if you have the green light to shoot anyone you don't recognize, how close did you come to shooting the guys I was with today?"

"First, is not a green light from anyone. I told the Luna men stay away, so I know I'm looking at an enemy. I kill someone from my side, morale goes to shit."

"I got you."

"But today, not close. I didn't have my weapon. And why would I shoot? We were just talking."

Marty said, "They all had guns pointed at you."

He saw the shoulders shrug in the window frame. "Just

for fun. They weren't going to shoot."

"Uh, that's not how it looked inside the truck."

"Who are they?" Maro asked.

"Yeah, it all came down pretty fast, them showing up. I wasn't hiding anything from you, it just, you know. Happened faster than I thought it would."

"I'm not upset. Just curious."

"Well, then get this," Marty said. "So I'm under a ton of pressure from my guys at Homeland to get some on-site security, right? I tell them yeah, you're right, but I keep stalling. Finally they tell me they'll freeze the contract if I don't get some, giving me some spiel about insurance and liability. So I call my buddy Hank, he runs operations for a company called Phalanx."

"Like the Greeks?" Maro said.

Marty was glad the lights were off, his mouth hanging open like that. "Yeah, the Greeks. You like history?"

"Tell your story, I want to hear it."

"Ah, so I tell Homeland I'll only use Phalanx, thinking I have some time before a crew will be available. Because here's the thing: all Hank's guys are busy in Iraq and Afghanistan, running VIPs around. But Hank screws me, says he can have boots on the ground here in a *day*. I'm like, Oh, that's *great*. Thanks a lot, man."

"So these men are professional security."

"Tier One, top of the line," Marty said.

"What should I know about them?"

"They're bad boys. You want details? Dave, get Maro copies of the files Hank sent us on Darwin and his guys. But Maro, it gets worse."

Dave said, "The whole files?"

"No, just the even pages. What do you think? The DD two-fourteens, all of it."

Dave shifted, the couch creaking under him. "I'll get them tomorrow." In Maro's direction: "The copier is in the trailer next door, where the crew's sleeping."

"No problem," Maro said. "His name is Darwin? The man I talked to?"

"That's right."

"I like his boots."

Marty frowned in the dark. "His *boots*?"

"You said it gets worse."

Marty didn't like the pace, this guy throwing curveballs then coming right down the middle. He took a breath, got it together and said, "I'm afraid so," like they were both getting screwed here. "The three-man team is temporary. Homeland wants complete coverage, and with Phalanx that means close protection for me at all times, three shooters to escort every vehicle, plus static crews for the job site."

"How many?"

"Hank told me between twelve and twenty-four guys, though he wasn't sure how soon he could get them here. They're still printing security money over in the cradle of civilization, so it's tough."

"I'll get things moved up."

"Maro, I can't move any faster on my end."

"I know, is okay. The security boys don't need to know what you doing, right? They just make sure you don't die."

"Yeah, but they aren't stupid."

Maro said, "That's good. If they smart, they do their jobs and keep their mouths shut. We can pay them extra to do their jobs extra good."

Marty didn't say anything, picturing what Darwin and his guys would do if they found out. If Marty put a stack of cash on the desk, told them to start shopping for fishing boats. He didn't know them very well, but had a feeling the cash would just sit there, all of them staring past it, right at him.

"These guys already make good money," he said, "so I don't know how far a bribe will go. I mean, guys at this level can make seven hundred a day, sometimes plus a per diem."

"That's not bad. Maybe I should make a résumé."

"Yeah, you'd be great. You know what's messed up? A

four-star general is worth about four-fifty a day."

"So they do this job for the money," Maro said. "Which means, to me, more money will work on them."

"Could be. We just have to be careful."

It was quiet for a few beats, then Maro said, "But it's good you bring all this up, for what I wanted to tell you today on the highway."

"Yeah?"

"The stuff we're bringing across next week."

"Okay. So?"

"It's tonight now, before dawn."

CHAPTER 7

DARWIN CHECKED HIS Suunto: About half past midnight, a little chilly and he wanted to get into the trailer for some sleep, but absolutely did not want to bend his knees to get up. Stupid, sitting here with your legs sticking out so they could get nice and stiff.

All right, just get it over with.

He pulled his feet in, wincing at the gravel between the bones, took a few Frankenstein steps while he scanned the area one last time. Going from the plane to the Suburban to this chair, he was surprised he could walk at all.

He started down the gentle slope to the trailers like he was barefoot on glass and paid attention to his two o'clock, over by Marty's trailer. He couldn't see the door from his lawn chair but had heard it open about an hour ago, Dave walking around the far corner toward the middle trailer and spooking something out the other way, maybe a hare or a real coyote, the black shape of it darting off.

Dave had climbed the steps to the middle trailer, pretty much straight ahead of Darwin's chair. He'd looked up and flinched, squinted into the dark until Darwin waved at him and Dave waved back, patted his heart and went inside.

Darwin looked for the animal, wanting it as an indicator that he'd been under the radar out there on watch, but it was gone. The feeling was gone too, the one like something was about to happen, though he was aware he'd felt it for a reason.

Just had to wait and see what it was, or go looking for it if it got worse.

●●●

In the trailer Darwin fought the breeze from Cal's snoring and woke him up by shaking his boot. Cal had come up swinging a few times, and if Gabe had been awake he and Darwin would Rock-Paper-Scissors to see who got to handle it. This time Cal just grunted awake and scratched his beard, looked for his sunglasses.

"You don't need them," Darwin said, low and with his back to Gabe's cot.

"Fah. Anything interesting?"

"Stars are nice. And maybe a real coyote to the west, so keep an eye out."

Cal stood up, stretched and touched the ceiling with his fingertips. "They in season?"

"I have no idea, but regardless, don't shoot any of them."

"Mm."

"Wear a coat. I put the chair up the hill, straight up from the middle trailer. Two hours, then get Gabe up. You two can leave around four thirty, I'll watch until everyone else rolls out."

Cal took the flashlight and radio from Darwin. He got his Sig off the card table, checked it, and slipped it into the thigh holster. He carried his coat in one hand and opened the door without a sound, whispered "Nightie night" to Darwin, and was gone.

Darwin put the .45 on the floor next to where his head would be, then bent over at the end of his cot and arm-walked his way flat onto it, told his knees they were welcome, and was asleep before they could answer.

●●●

Maro had everyone in place by three a.m., coming down out of the Mexico hills to the bank of the Rio where they crouched in the scrub and tried to hear over the water. Maro did another head count: Arturo, one of his officers, the twelve *mujado* farmers or whatever they were with the huge backpacks stuffed with marijuana, and the four salvajes to guard them and give them a shove if necessary.

He didn't think it would be. These guys were chomping to get across the border and there was a good chance they'd just keep going, which Maro didn't care about—there were always more—but they were all dumb enough to get arrested and he couldn't have them talking about what was going on here.

Maro looked the men over, told them, "Don't think about your families right now. Think about getting across and back without doing anything stupid."

He had at least one member of each man's family in a village about half an hour away by truck along with more *salvajes*, told these men if they acted up he'd have the church walls painted with the hostages' blood. He'd shown them pictures of another house in Juárez where it had happened, the images good and sharp, taken by a reporter from *El Diario*. They'd just looked at the photos and nodded, didn't say anything when he told them the police decided it was best to burn the place down after the two-day investigation was over.

Now one of the men was praying to himself, asking Jesus

to watch over his *abuela* in the house. Arturo had come here from the house and said she was a cranky old bean, always hollering and refusing to eat anything.

Maro listened to the muttering for a few seconds, turned to the man and said, "You want me to call the house, have her throat cut while you listen?"

"No."

"Because then you won't have to pray for her anymore."

"No."

"Okay. Be quiet then. Pray in your head, Jesus can still hear it."

He turned back to the river and waited. The man kept quiet. Maro could see the Lindy construction site across the water and up the hill, that one light giving everything a clean, cold look. He told the *mujado* farmers again: stay to the right, around the flat area for the tower and the shipping box, down in the shallow arroyo that brought rainwater down to the river. It was the only way to stay hidden going up the hill without jumping from bush to bush. They nodded, their eyes big and shining.

This was a test run to see how well the gravel and pipes Marty's men had put in the river worked. They said this was the best spot, where the current was right and the brown water would hide it all in the aerial view. If it was good, Maro would let the cartel know they could send four-wheelers through his area, then maybe trucks.

That was the cartel's plan, anyway.

Maro nodded to Arturo, who tapped one of the *salvajes* and the two of them eased through the brush to the water's edge and looked, listened, then waded in. They found the gravel path with the pipes underneath it to let the water through. Arturo looked back and gave a thumbs-up, then he and the *salvaje* walked across the Rio, their feet barely under the water.

Maro turned to the praying man and said, smiling, "Hey, you want to pray to Jesus, look, there he is. Two of him."

•••

Gabe woke Darwin up at four in the morning, the sleep falling right off and leaving him feeling like he'd only been on the cot for ten minutes.

"I need a shower," he said.

Gabe nudged Cal's foot on his way to the card table and Cal said, "I'm up, dammit."

They got up and around, stretching and popping, the windows showing black outside.

Darwin headed for the bathroom. "If anything blows up outside, come get me when you hear the water stop."

He stood under the shower, as hot as it would go but not nearly hot enough, though the pressure was decent. There was a cracked bar of Irish Spring on a little formed shelf, no shampoo, so he used the soap for everything. He came out smelling fresh and wearing clean khaki 5.11 Taclite pants and his short-sleeved charcoal shirt, the level III armor underneath, everything tucked and tight and feeling good.

"Stand back," Cal said, "he's got his tactical pants on."

Darwin said, "How long until Marty has some 5.11 airlifted in, maybe some Oakley wraparounds?"

Gabe was packing a go bag on the table, identification and spare magazines and one of the med kits. "You see him checking out my watch? He'd look at it, then down at the dinky little thing he has on, like now it doesn't tell time good enough."

"He wants to be on tactical time," Darwin said. He got the .45 strapped to his thigh, jumped up and down, everything secure. "So what should we call him over comms?"

Cal stopped at the bathroom door. "Shit, you know he wants to be Viper."

"Reaper," Gabe said.

Darwin thought it over. "Nah, I think he'll go prestigious. Something like Sultan. Or War Admiral."

"War Admiral?" Gabe said. "Isn't that a horse?"

"He's rich. They love horses."

Gabe frowned, found it reasonable. "Well, if that's what he wants."

"No, no," Cal said, "it doesn't matter what he *wants*. He gets what he gets, and if he doesn't like it, tough shit." He closed the door and the shower kicked on.

Darwin looked at Gabe and they both grinned, starting to get Cal riled on call signs, pretty much the only thing that got under his skin.

Through the wall Cal said, "Yeah, keep smiling, assholes."

●●●

Gabe had the laptop going, said to Darwin, "Tracking has the package on schedule." He saw his wife was online, just past 6 a.m. in Detroit, and started chatting with her.

Darwin grabbed the go bag and the Suburban keys and stepped out of the trailer, not even a hint of the sun coming up yet.

He listened, could barely hear the river flowing at the bottom of the hill. There was a definite bite in the air, the open sky letting all the heat out. He checked for that feeling, the coiled spring close by, but got nothing.

The Suburban was parked up the hill on a semi-flat spot big enough to turn around in, and as Darwin unlocked it and dropped the go bag into the passenger footwell he made a note to mention they should park facing the way out, case they were in a hurry.

He started the engine and got the heater going, hit the

lights and watched them spill over the landscape and get lost when they shot over the gulley to the southeast, out past the tower site.

•••

Maro froze when he heard the vehicle start, looked over at Arturo and almost laughed when the lights came on and Arturo's face was shown to be so surprised. They ducked further into the gulley and waited, listening, then one of the *mujado* farmers bolted back toward the river.

Maro had his biggest *salvaje* back there and he snagged the farmer's bulky pack as he went past and pulled him to the ground and put an elbow on his throat. He looked at Maro in the light that filtered down through the mesquite branches along the arroyo's ridge.

Maro watched the farmer to see if he kept fighting. He didn't, just lay there with his hands almost touching the arm that was choking him. Maro nodded, gestured to let him up. The *salvaje* stepped back toward the river, ready in case the farmer tried again.

He didn't. He rolled onto his side and pulled his knees up to his chest, slowly kept going until he was on his knees with his eyes on the ground. Maro looked at the *salvaje* and flicked his own ear. The *salvaje* pulled his knife and slashed the farmer across his left ear, a quick stroke, to mark him so Maro could pick him out later.

Maro looked up at the light beams cutting over the top of the arroyo. They weren't moving, and the sound of the vehicle didn't race or get closer. It was sitting still. He looked down the arroyo and memorized the shape of the farmer, his outline, and would look for him if they had to run from *la migra*; police, the Border Patrol, or Marty's new elite security force. Maro would stab the man in the lungs or shoot him if noise was okay, so maybe the police would stop and try to save him while the rest got away.

●●●

Gabe didn't trust the size of the trailer's water heater, pushed his shower to when they got back. Cal sniffed in his direction and made a face, Gabe telling him, "Please. All you smell through that raccoon on your face is last night's dinner."

Cal patted his beard. "Don't listen to him."

Darwin hit Send on an email to Hank at the Phalanx office in Baghdad, letting him know about the possible contact yesterday and making sure they were cleared with Homeland and Border to be operating in the area. He hoped the guys in the Jeep weren't some kind of undercover immigration unit, off the radar and looking for trouble.

They all compared phone battery and signal levels, then Gabe and Cal checked their side arms, strapped them down and headed out the door. Darwin followed them to the Suburban and patted Cal's passenger windowsill.

"Remember, you get the chance, see if these beasts are the vehicle of choice for unsavories around here. If all the cartel honchos drive 'em, we ought to get some spray paint. Or armor."

They nodded.

"Also, snacks: Protein, and some Gatorade to keep our salt up. How much ammo did we pack in the case?"

Gabe said, "Few hundred rounds. But it's that shit we got from the dealer in Kuwait."

"Oh yeah." Darwin remembered him, selling ammunition right next to bootleg DVDs and boxed TGIF appetizers that should have been in a freezer. "You see an open gun shop, pick up some more. Quality, we don't want anything curving around to hit us in the ass. And hey, look at me."

They both did, Cal's sunglasses up in his hair.

Darwin forked two fingers at his eyes, then theirs. "Fucking *pan*cakes."

They took off. Darwin listened to the engine get quieter until it was gone, looked up at the stars and wondered when the sun would decide to punch in. He took two steps toward the lawn chair before he realized the feeling was back, telling him: Wait, here it comes.

• • •

Maro waited ten minutes after the vehicle was gone before he moved again, easing up the slope of the arroyo to take a look at the trailers past the flat tower site that was bright in the starlight, almost like snow. The shipping box was there too, a dark shape about the size of a semi trailer, but he couldn't think about it—what was inside it—right now. No point in getting angry unless he had to.

No one moved around the trailers, in or out, all the windows dark. Maro scanned the scrub brush uphill from the buildings, looking for the lawn chair he'd seen after he left Marty's trailer, Dave acting as a distraction. He couldn't see it, but knew it was there and someone was in it.

Which one?

Maybe the stocky Mexican-looking one, or the one with the Mujahideen beard.

Or the one from the Suburban window, Patrick Darwin, Marty said, then later told him the man's codename, or call sign, Sheepdog. The dog who smiled at Maro over the sights of his .45 and cursed at him, practically spitting in his face.

Let it be him, Maro thought, so the next time he's smiling, tell him: Hey Sheepdog, I like your lawn chair, especially from behind.

Watch the smile drop off his face.

Maro knew the meaning behind the name. Marty was the sheep, the men who wanted to grab or shoot him were wolves, and this Darwin man was the thing between them, keeping the wolves away.

Maro liked the name; it defined him as a wolf, *lobo*, which sounded right. Though he could be a snake or a scorpion, a falcon, even a shark, whatever was necessary.

He got the farmers with their giant packs moving up the arroyo, their small sounds confined below the ridgeline. At the top of the hill the walls would get shorter until it was just a ditch, then flat land. By then they would be behind the lawn chair and Maro would have to worry about other things, but for now he liked concentrating on the man in the chair, the Sheepdog, almost wishing he'd spot the wolf so Maro could see what he'd do.

CHAPTER 8

DARWIN SPOTTED ALL of them, eventually.

He was using wide-angle vision, not really focusing on one thing, turning his head from side to side and letting his peripherals pick up on movement when something out on his left blocked the sky that was showing between two blots of darkness, either rocks or bushes.

Then it was gone, the sky and horizon showing again.

Darwin didn't turn his head. Staring at it in the dark would make it harder to see or turn it into something else, his mind trying to put a label on it. He kept his eyes ahead but concentrated on that corner of his vision as another shape moved through the space.

Deer?

He didn't know if Texas had them.

Didn't every state?

The shapes were moving uphill, toward his seven or eight o'clock. He hit Cal's number on the phone.

Cal said, "Let me guess: waffles."

"Are there deer in Texas?" Darwin spoke low, his forearm in front of his mouth to keep the sound from traveling.

"Deer? Yeah, whitetail, mule deer. Antelope. Why?"

"I might have something here. I got shapes moving up the hill from the tower site, probably through the gulley we saw out there."

"You want us to turn around?"

Darwin thought about it. They'd been gone fifteen, twenty minutes, could probably get back in ten if they had to. Whatever was out there, it would be gone "Maybe just pull over. I'll call you back."

"Pulling over," Cal said. "Leave the line open. I want to hear you try to sneak around."

Darwin zipped the phone into his chest pocket and stood up, ignored the pain and bent his knees until they were done popping. He pulled the .45 and moved uphill in a crouch, angling toward where the shapes would be if they kept on the same line. The ground was hard but quiet.

He could picture Gabe and Cal in the Suburban, looking for a spot to turn around on the two-track with the phone on the console between them, listening to him breathing.

If it is a bunch of deer, he told himself, and they spook this way, don't fucking yell. He kept on the angled line and every few seconds would stop, listen. He could hear footsteps and what sounded like fabric moving on fabric.

He moved over the crest of the hill and kept scrub brush at his rear to make sure he wasn't skylined for anybody who might be off to his left. The top of the gulley was maybe fifty yards away, at his two o'clock. He went to one knee and got back into wide-angle, his head moving in a slow scan.

There.

What would be funny, get the phone out and ask Cal if any Texas deer wore cowboy hats. Instead he pulled his jacket up to his face and whispered through the fabric, "Got people. Gulley past the tower site. Hostility unknown. Standby."

Darwin went over the possibilities. If they're illegals, best thing would be to shoo them back across and report it. Babysitting a bunch of sad folks until Border showed up, no thanks. Might have a *coyote* with them, somebody armed, but they'd likely scoot at any sign of trouble, leave the people behind or try another spot tomorrow night.

But if they were drug runners, or somebody looking to give Marty trouble, they'd be up for a fight. Darwin eased the pocket zipper open, got his phone out and said, "I'm at the top of the hill. Count to thirty, then yell something. Orders."

"Copy," Cal said. "En route."

Darwin turned the phone's volume all the way up and put it on speaker, set it on a rock that came up to his calf. He moved to his left, fast but soft, away from the top of the hill. He wanted an angle on the people coming out of the gulley, him and them and the phone making three points on a right triangle.

He stopped and knelt and hit thirty in his head.

Some kind of words blew out of his phone, then sharp movement to his direct front and he had time to mark the group further along than he'd thought when from forty yards away someone opened up with an AK-47, the crack and blowback unmistakable, and Darwin dropped to the ground.

He could see the muzzle flash through the scrub, blossoming out to the right toward the phone. Darwin fired four times at the spot to the left of the flash, the.45 punching into the darkness, then he was up and moving backward toward the parking area. He watched for the muzzle flash to go again, this time flat, fanning out to each side telling him the AK was pointed his way.

He heard people running, crashing through the gulley toward the Rio. He stayed put, letting them go. If the guy with the AK was with them, super. If he was waiting for the guy with the .45 to chase them, run right through his field of fire, he could go fuck himself.

Down the hill Darwin heard a trailer door slap open. Somebody yelled, "What the hell is going on?"

Goddammit.

Darwin yelled, "Go back inside, get—"

The AK opened up again, pocking the ground to his left and dragging this way.

Darwin fired twice and moved back, trying to break

contact. Now he had the trailers downhill at his three o'clock. If he kept moving back and pulled the AK with him, he'd drop it right on top of the trailers, maybe force the guy to run down there and barricade himself inside.

Well, no more moving back.

He started working out a maneuver to his left, flank the AK and come up on him for close-up work. Tough to do on a quiet night with nothing else to hold the guy's attention. Maybe if he had the night vision gear that was packed with the long guns.

Sit tight, Darwin told himself. Gabe and Cal are on the way.

He knelt behind a rock that would give cover if he tried hard enough, became part of its shape and waited. The phone thing might have been a mistake. Now it was up there between him and the AK, and if the other guy got hold of it he could cause trouble. Call Hank and tell him in Spanish his guys couldn't shoot. Or call Christine, then probably surrender.

Movement pulled his eyes to the right, out past the tower site, and he could see shapes running where the gulley opened up to flow into the Rio. Please, he thought, somebody down there shoot an AK up in the air in celebration.

Didn't happen.

But he did hear a vehicle coming fast, the Suburban. Good and bad. Chances were they'd roll in hard, bright lights and loud noises, looking to spook anybody who shouldn't be around. Could work, but they'd silhouette Darwin for anybody out there.

He looked back and saw the headlight beams bouncing up and down, the guys about a mile out. He got ready to move again, this time toward his nine o'clock, but stopped when he heard a guy with an accent say, "Patrick Darwin, is that you?"

● ● ●

Darwin was pissed at first, thinking it was his phone, somebody getting on the line and using real names. He shook that off within a second and tried to process this guy with an AK in the Texas desert knowing his name. The guy's voice was close, thirty yards out.

Darwin eased down closer to his rock. "Who's that?" he said.

"You don't remember me?"

Christ, was this somebody he'd worked with before? It had happened back in Delta, train some "elite" foreign troops and end up shooting at them six months later after a military coup.

So, what, the guy recognized the sound of your gun? Don't be an idiot, you know who it is.

"Hey, my Jeep buddy."

"That's right. How are you?"

Closer now. The guy was moving like a cat. Keep it short.

"Good, you?" Darwin moved back in a crouch. If the guy went for the trailers he'd drop him in the light.

"I'm upset. You making me look bad out here in front of my men."

"Well, I didn't know it was you." He sidestepped to the left, low and quiet.

"I call you next time." Sounded like the guy was smiling. What kind of accent was that? Not Mexican. Darwin could see the headlight beams from the Suburban cutting across the top of the scrub in front of him. That put it on the last straightaway before the parking area, less than half a mile.

Darwin said, "Hey, you wearing a cowboy hat now?"

No answer. He kept his ears tuned ahead for movement, let his eyes relax and find the shapes for him. The bushes and rocks up there could all be hiding someone. Those big prickly pear leaves could be a shoulder hunched down, a head peeking out at him.

"Hey Patrick," the guy said. "Or you go by Sheepdog when you shooting?"

You gotta be kidding me, Darwin thought. "What's your name?"

"*Lobo.*"

"Good one."

"I'm the wolf, you the dog. Hey *perro*, why don't you find another job?"

The guy was matching his steps, staying in front of him. Darwin stopped moving. "I'm pretty good at this one."

"Me too. Better than you."

"You think so?"

"We gonna see."

Darwin fired twice, moved, fired twice more and dropped the magazine out with one round left in the chamber. He pulled the next mag and slid it in, his hands knowing what to do in the dark. He ran to his left, the timing good enough as the Suburban came over the last little hill and splashed its headlights over the area, shadows dancing and jumping. Darwin found a small depression that stayed black in the headlights and he ran to it, spun and dropped on his belly to look past the .45 at where this guy was.

The shadows made it hard but he couldn't see anybody moving. Gabe pushed the Suburban into the brush as far as he could and Darwin heard the doors open.

Gabe said, "Sheepdog."

"At your ten o'clock. AK at your twelve, maybe forty yards out, trying to get to the river. I'm off comms."

"Copy," Gabe said. "Moving to your nine."

Darwin knew what the guys were doing without having to see it. He and Gabe would handle all the shouting over the Suburban's engine while Cal moved just below the crest of the hill and sprinted to flank the AK, get between him and the river and wait. For as big as he was, Cal could move like a snake.

Gabe said to the bushes around him, "You two, sweep around and get into that gully. Everybody else, skirmish line, move up."

Darwin grinned in his little foxhole. The headlights made a pattern of long shadows out of the bushes and he rolled to the nearest one and popped into a crouch, moved forward in the pattern until he was at the rock he'd met earlier. He looked out where he'd seen the shapes running toward the river and now could pick out distinct features and the water, a dark ribbon sliding by. Above it, across the border, the hills were showing color.

Darwin looked east. The sun was coming up.

The gulley ahead was still a black gash. The AK was either in there and moving toward Cal or through it and out the other side. Darwin covered while Gabe moved across the flat ground at the mouth of the gulley. No AK fire.

"Pretty open over here," Gabe said from the other side of the brush that ran along the gulley's rims.

"Don't put him behind you."

"Nothing back there to hide behind," Gabe said, letting Darwin know the guy had to be in the gulley.

"Moving." Darwin stayed low, got up to the rock where he'd left his phone. The ground was pocked and the rock showed three hits from the AK's first burst. His phone was fine. "Back on comms," he said, wanting the guy to fire his way while the rock was right there. Let Gabe and Cal drop in on him and get this over with.

Nothing happened.

"Moving," Gabe said, and Darwin covered the black gulley and waited for the muzzle flash.

●●●

Darwin and Gabe swept along the sides of the gulley, squeezing it like a tube of toothpaste toward Cal, enough light now to see the sand and rocks down at the bottom. The ground was all messed up and showed damp sand on top of dry from all the people running around. They were almost to the bottom of the hill when a clump of scrub said, "I think it's clear."

Cal stood up out of it but kept his Sig ready. Darwin looked past him where the land nearly flattened out before it hit the Rio. More tracks, rocks kicked over. Across the gulley, just a ditch at this point, Gabe scanned the area behind him, came back and looked at Darwin. He tilted his head back up the gulley.

Darwin nodded and checked with Cal, who dropped into a tight crouch and moved into the gulley, Sig up. Darwin and Gabe started back up the hill to catch anything he flushed out. They went ten steps before Cal said, "Stop. Got an IED."

Darwin looked across at Gabe and they gave each other the same face: Really?

"Coming in," Darwin said. He looped back around to follow Cal's path and came up to him kneeling a few yards away from two bigger rocks that would let one man pass at a time if they didn't climb over. Sticks and a few pieces of trash were piled against the uphill side of the rocks.

On the downhill side a hand grenade was wedged between one of the big rocks and a smaller one that had been set there. The smaller rock was pressing against the grenade's spoon, keeping the thing from going off. A fresh-cut stick angled across the path so someone coming downhill would kick it and move the smaller rock, release the spoon and get his ass blown off.

Darwin leaned in. "Is that a South Korean grenade?"

"Ding ding," Cal said. "I'd known we're fighting Korea too, I woulda brought my tactical pants."

"Huh," Darwin said. "You see the pin anywhere?"

"Asshole took it with him. Or tossed it on his way across. Dude's gone." He stared at the grenade, turned and looked across the Rio. "Probably went home to get his fucking bazooka."

●●●

Darwin holstered the .45 and walked toward the trailers, the four workers and Marty standing out in the chilly morning air watching him. Marty had on a parka made for Alpine skiing, his hair poking out of the hood. The workers had coffee mugs, steam rising up to their faces while they nudged each other and pointed up the hill trying to figure out what had happened.

"Morning," Darwin said. "Everybody okay? Where's Dave?"

Marty was ready to act out, had to hold up and say, "He's fine, he's making breakfast." Then he put his arms out. "What the hell are you guys doing?"

Darwin ignored him and looked at the workers. "You got any rope I can borrow?"

One of them, a Nordic-looking guy with huge hands, said, "How strong?"

"We gotta yank on a stick to blow up a grenade." That got them going.

"A grenade?" Marty said. "Why'd you bring one of those?"

"We didn't, somebody left it for us. Nice, huh?"

Darwin left Marty standing there with his mouth open and walked with the Nordic guy, who turned out to be a structural engineer named Jim, to the red Conex. Jim used a crowded keychain to pop the lock, worked the lever handles and swung the doors open. It was cold inside and smelled like an oil change shop. Darwin identified welding and cutting tools, shovels and picks and posthole diggers, some scaffold strapped against the far wall, but everything else was new to him or hidden in yellow and orange hard plastic cases.

"Hey," he said, "you guys ever work with explosives?"

"Sorry, we call in another company for that kinda thing. Hoping we'd get rid of that grenade for you?"

"You want it, it's all yours."

Jim checked to see if he was serious.

"Not really," Darwin said. "I just need the rope."

Jim pointed at a wall of pegs and hooks dripping with mountain climbing gear. "Take your pick."

Darwin grabbed a coil of 8mm blue and red cord. "This okay?"

"A fine choice," Jim said, and Darwin caught a whiff of something under the oil and coffee, maybe vodka, the guy either hungover or drinking already today. It disappointed Darwin for a few seconds before he told himself to stop being an asshole, judging the guy like that.

He hefted the cord. "You guys climb?"

"We had to get certified for the job, rappelling into crevasses or climbing to get rock samples or whatever. Some of the guys do it for fun. I'm not one of them."

Walking back Darwin knew Jim wanted to ask about the gunshots and grenade but was trying to be cool about it. Darwin didn't want to say anything until he'd had a chance to talk to Cal and Gabe about how his pal with the AK knew his name and call sign. Maybe ask Marty about it too. The silence was getting to the point where Jim was going to say something so Darwin said, "All you guys engineers?"

"Yeah, structural. Eric and Brad are also master electricians. John, the one over there with his hardhat already on, has a Master's in computer science."

"Man," Darwin said.

"Thought all we did was move dirt around, huh?"

"When you aren't taking coffee breaks."

"Nah, Marty's got that covered."

"He a good guy to work for?"

Jim looked up, made sure they were far enough away. "Pay is good. Long as he stays in his trailer, everything's fine. Every now and then he comes out, messes shit up, and we have to wait for him to go back inside before we fix it."

"Sounds like most of the bosses I've had. We called 'em officers."

Jim said, "Marty told us he worked with you guys over in Iraq."

"We guarded some of his people, Lindy Construction people, and some sites. But I never met him before this."

"The way he told it, everybody over there was trying to kill him."

"Well, that's nothing special. Just being a foreigner, they'd try to get you." They were getting close to the group, Marty turning around and putting his hands on his hips, that coat making him look like the Michelin man.

Jim kept his voice low, said, "Hey, you think if those insurgents had met Marty, spent some time with him, they would have tried a little harder?"

•••

Darwin was on his belly next to Cal, who'd tied the cord around the stick, whistling, then left a few coils of slack next to it and fed about three hundred feet of cord out as he walked toward the Rio. Now they were behind a rock about the size of a clothes basket. Behind the blue Conex next to the tower site would be better, but the angle was bad.

Darwin looked over his shoulder at the hills across the border, came back and squinted up the gulley toward the booby trap. "You think he's watching us?"

"Fuck yeah he is, and laughing his ass off. Coupla clowns

lying in the dirt. I hope he doesn't have a sniper rifle."

"I thought we had him no problem. We ran it right, and not only does he slip through, he has time to set *this* up."

"I think we got us a bona fide badass."

"Get this: he knows my name."

Cal stared at him through his Maui Jims. "Say huh?"

"Called me by my full name. Then my goddam call sign."

Cal looked at the cord in his hands, up toward the grenade. "Who the fuck is this guy?"

"I was thinking I might've worked with him before, back in Delta, that's why he was so surprised when I rolled my window down yesterday. Maybe he recognized me."

"But you don't remember him?"

"Not at all," Darwin said. "And I think his accent is *Cuban*. I sure as shit never trained any Cubans."

They stopped talking to watch Marty, about a hundred yards away, step away from the group and cup his hands around his mouth.

"Incoming bullshit," Cal said.

Marty yelled, "What's taking so long?"

Darwin waved him back toward the group, said to Cal, "He makes it worse. Our badass buddy is watching us, now we're lying in the dirt taking orders from that clown."

"Well Patrick," Cal said, "In my years of experience, I've found if I just worry about impressing myself, everything else falls into place."

"Is that right?"

"Quite." Cal pushed to one knee, yelled, "Fire in the hole!" and dropped back down as he yanked the cord. They counted the seconds together, one, two, three, and felt the ground jump along with the flat *whump*. Darwin took a peek, saw the dust cloud drifting out of the gulley. Jim and the engineers clapped like it was fireworks. Darwin stood up, his knees griping about all the running and crouching.

They walked toward the group while Cal pulled the cord into a coil, saying "Lookit," when he saw the stick was still tied to the other end. He pulled it in and handed the coil to Darwin so he could untie the knot, the stick a little scraped up but solid.

"I'm keeping this," Cal said.

•••

Darwin gave the cord to Jim. "Much appreciated." To the group: "Now, I'm sure it would have come up before now, but I have to ask. Is that the first grenade you guys have come across out here?"

"First grenade," Marty said, ticking off his fingers, "first automatic gunfire, first threat of any kind. This is a good racket you got going. Everything's fine, we bring in security and shit starts blowing up. What now? Wait, I got it: More security."

Darwin said, "How was everything fine, everybody trying to capture or kill you?"

"I'm saying nothing happened until you guys got here."

"So we were just in time," Cal said.

Marty gave him a flat look, saw he was going to lose this one. "Shouldn't you have kept the grenade? For evidence?"

Cal tapped his stick against his thigh. "The way it was rigged, I try to save that bugger there'd be little bits of my evidence all over the landscape."

"Well, they're gonna be pissed."

"Who?" Darwin said.

"Border Patrol," Marty said. "Hello, I called it in a half hour ago."

"Marty, you gotta tell me that stuff. Somebody comes over that hill with a shotgun, guess how that conversation goes? Next time let me call it in."

"Hey, I'm just trying to help. You guys got your

paperwork squared away? They're gonna check it."

"In the trailer," Darwin said, happy for a reason to walk away. He and Cal left the group standing there and got to the end of their trailer that faced the Rio. It was still chilly in the shade. Darwin looked out across the land and water to Mexico, said, "See anything good?"

From the darkness under the trailer Gabe still had the binoculars up, watching the hills.

He said, "You guys are gonna love this."

●●●

Gabe stayed under the trailer and told them about the two guys he'd been watching in the hills, both of them sitting in the morning sun with mugs of something, passing a set of binoculars back and forth to watch the action on this side of the border.

"What do they look like?" Darwin said.

"Too far out for dental records," Gabe said, "but one of 'em's our boy from the Jeep. They're over there nudging each other, laughing it up, and when Cal blew the grenade our buddy stood up and took a bow."

"I knew it," Cal said. "Fucker."

Darwin asked, "He have an AK with him?"

"Not that I can see. We need a spotting scope."

"Probably waiting for us at the airport by now," Cal said.

Darwin checked his watch. "They looking this way?"

"They are now," Gabe said. "Keeping track of *you* though. I'm a ghost under here."

"Keep an eye on them for a bit. They just sit there doing nothing for the next fifteen, crawl out the back. Border's on the way, I don't want them seeing you sneaking around in the dirt. Might think we're up to something."

"Are we?" Cal said.

Darwin looked out at the hills, hoping the guy was looking right at him. "This guy keeps pushing, I think we will be."

CHAPTER 9

MARTY MET THE Border Patrol truck in the parking area and brought the two agents down to the trailers. Darwin sipped his coffee and waited for them in his lawn chair, which he'd moved to the back side of Marty's trailer. He felt like he was getting in trouble and didn't want anybody on the other side of the Rio to see it. He'd told Cal and Gabe to wait in their trailer and let Hank know what was going on; if Border didn't need to talk to them, great.

The agents looked like a before and after photo, one tall and solid, the other small, shorter than Marty and lean. They had dark green cargo uniforms and matching baseball caps, sunglasses, gear hanging off their belts and shoulders.

They got close and Marty said, "This is the guy you're looking for, but don't arrest him if you don't have to. Pat, I explained what you and your guys are doing here, helping me out."

Darwin stood up and put his hand out to the big guy but the small one grabbed it and shook and Darwin felt the slender hand, saw the blond ponytail coming out the back of the hat.

"How are you sir," she said, "I'm Lead Border Patrol Agent Anna Ricks, this is Border Patrol Agent Brian Molina."

"Patrick Darwin, nice to meet you guys."

She was maybe thirty, hard to tell behind the glasses that took up half her face but she made them work. He shook hands with Molina, who was Hispanic and had a face that looked about nineteen.

Marty stood behind the agents and waited for Darwin to look at him, then raised his eyebrows, checked out her ass and nodded. "Pat, this is the agent I mentioned yesterday, works out of the state park?"

She nodded at Marty, turned back and said, "We hear you had an interesting morning."

"Yeah, I thought Texas was supposed to be friendly. Where's the Southern hospitality?" See if she had a sense of humor about it.

"Southern hospitality has been officially suspended within ten miles of the border," she said with a straight face.

"Oo," Marty said. "Was I right about her?"

Darwin kept his eyes on her. "You want the play-by-play?"

"First, I'm going to assume you have all the necessary licenses for performing security operations in the state of Texas."

"You assume correct," Darwin said, bowing his head.

"Firearms fully documented?"

"Whatever you need." Darwin smiled at Molina, who was staring at the .45.

"We're going to have to check anyway," she said, "but I wanted to hear it from you first. You're lacking any of that, we'd let you tell it to the judge."

"I understand," Darwin said.

That out of the way, she crossed her arms and leaned toward him, telling secrets. "Okay, so what happened?"

●●●

Darwin walked them through it, showed them the phone rock and bullet marks, scooped his empty magazine out of the dirt and let them look at it, sniff it. He told them about the highway encounter but left out the part about the guy knowing his name. He still wasn't sure what to do with that.

They collected his brass in a plastic bag. When he was done with his side of the story, they walked toward the gulley and found brass from the AK scattered around and collected that too.

Anna said, "So they're moving through here, out of the gulley when your guy. . ."

"Cal," Darwin said.

"Cal yells through the phone and this guy opens fire with an automatic weapon, an AK-47."

"That's right," Darwin said. "Look here, you can see where he came out of the gulley to move toward me after the initial burst."

Molina squatted next to the spot, eyeballed the tracks and turned his head to follow them toward the parking area. Marty leaned on his knees and did the same, stood up and said, "Did anybody check the Suburban for holes?"

"That's a good idea," Anna said. "If you see any, don't touch them, just keep count."

Marty frowned. "Okay, well, I've got some things to do but I'll send Dave up, tell him to report back to you."

"I'll be expecting him."

Marty picked his way down the hill to his trailer. When he was out of earshot Darwin said, "That was very smooth."

"He was stepping all over everything." She shook her head. "Least we can tell which tracks are his; nobody else wears loafers out here. And I'm used to guys checking out my ass, but please. I'm armed. Some subtlety would be nice."

"Oh, you have an ass?"

"Keep it up," she said.

Darwin checked with Molina, making sure he wasn't

sneaking in between the two of them, get on the wrong side of the guy. Molina was crawling through the brush into the gulley, making a racket. Then Darwin thought about Christine for a few seconds, not feeling bad but wondering what she'd do, she saw him flirting with this woman. Roll her eyes and hand him the divorce papers she'd had written up without talking to him about it.

"What do you carry?" Darwin asked Anna.

"H&K P2000, forty cal," she said.

"Huh."

She held up the bag of his .45 brass. "I'm supposed to be impressed?"

"Hey, I'm not judging you. I just like knowing what I hit goes down and stays there."

She made a show of turning in a circle, checking behind a rock. "What exactly did you hit?"

"I'd like my lawyer now."

"That's what I thought." She hooked her thumbs in her belt and surveyed the area, said, "You're sure it was just one guy firing."

"One's enough. And yes, I'm sure."

"And another ten or so besides him, who all ran."

"Somewhere around there."

She thought about it. "One armed guy, to me, means it could be a few things. Illegals coming in with a guide, but the crossers usually surrender, just happy to get some food and water. I'm leaning toward a small drug run or a weapons pickup."

"Weapons going over the border?"

"Big time," she said. "Houston's the main supply, but these guys can go into any gun store, buy in bulk, and sell it all to the cartels. You might have run across a pickup, one armed escort running a bunch of mules to a meet. He buys the guns and the other guys carry them back."

"Seems labor intensive."

"Hey, they got all the cheap manual labor they need.

Those hills across the Rio, up to Juárez, down to Torreón and all the way east to pretty much the Gulf, that's all Luna Cartel territory. To them, everybody who lives there is a volunteer. And I'm sure if you asked the Luna boys, they'd tell you this is their land too, this side of the border."

"I kinda got that feeling," Darwin said. "Pisses me off a little."

"They hire mercenaries to run some of the crews, guys who don't want power, just money."

Darwin caught the tone. She'd timed it right—he had to squint toward the sun and a bit uphill to look at her. Since when did he give up the high ground so easily? "We aren't mercenaries."

"Did I say that?" She crossed her arms and he hoped they weren't done playing around already.

He said, "Who you think has more money, the Luna Cartel or Martin Lindy?"

"Luna probably owns a few companies like Marty's just so they can play with the trucks."

"Right. So if we were mercenaries, we'd be on the other side of the border right now."

"Have they made you an offer?"

"Yeah, they're talking to my agent right now."

She said, "Well, you've been here what, less than a day?"

He stopped, saw she was serious. "Wait, did they try to buy you?"

"Offered enough money to retire on, said if I turned it down they'd pay for my funeral."

"Come on."

"Anybody over here in a uniform gets the same offer eventually, so I didn't feel too special. What got to me is how they delivered it. They called my parents in *Ohio* and told them to pass it along."

Darwin looked across the border, wishing he'd kept her out of sight from the hills over there. If the guys watching recognized her . . . He came back and looked at the gun on her hip and the little smile she had, talking about this drug cartel calling her folks with death threats.

Christ, he thought. Don't let this girl know you want to protect her. She'll kick your ass.

Molina walked up through the gulley and came out onto the flatter ground at the top. "Tracks in there are deep. Those guys were weighted down."

"Drug run," Anna said.

Darwin wanted to talk more about the threats but would leave it up to her in front of Molina. "Is this good news?"

"Not really," she said. "They poke at one spot on the border, see if they can get through. They can't, they'll try another spot, sometimes less than a mile away." She shook her head. "This is a weird spot to pick though. River's a bitch, plus Marty's crap here big as all get-out."

Darwin said, "You're the first law enforcement I've seen here so far. Could be the reason they picked it."

"Could be. But man, you're risking your life in the current down there. Safer places, we have heavy patrols. Boats, ATVs, helicopters."

Sticking up for the uniform, Darwin thought. "Sounds like you pushed them out into no-man's."

She nodded, looked at Molina. "You have plans tonight?"

"I did."

"I got a better offer. Sitting out here with me in the dark and cold."

"How can I say no to that?"

Darwin thought: Why would you?

Anna said to him, "Looks like we're in your neighborhood tonight."

"Not a problem. How can we help?"

"Just stay out of the way, no offense. If you can go get deputized before tonight, that's a different story."

Darwin almost mentioned the crate of weapons they'd have before the sun went down, decided to keep that to himself for now.

Anna took another look around, said, "Hey, Marty mentioned something about you guys blowing up evidence?"

●●●

Darwin walked them back from the grenade site toward the trailers, Gabe and Cal standing there looking up at the clouds and pointing at things. Gabe had a black binder under one arm. If it was two males from Border out here, Darwin thought, those two would still be inside lying low. Cal even had his good hat on, the khaki American flag with the tunnel brim.

Darwin introduced Anna and Molina, told them, "This is Gabe, former law enforcement in Detroit, and Cal. He used to be a synchronized swimmer."

"You handled the grenade?" Anna said.

"That's right, Miss."

Darwin glanced at Gabe, got a twitched eyebrow from him. Cal had a plan here. Darwin put his hands in his pockets and waited to see if he'd step on this landmine.

Anna said, "Off the record, we appreciate that. Saves us sitting here all day babysitting that thing while a bomb squad tries to read a map."

"Not a problem. If there's anything else I can help you remove, I'd be more than happy." He grinned, his teeth white in that beard.

Jesus, Darwin thought.

Anna nodded. "I need somebody skilled at yanking once and exploding, I'll find you."

Cal looked at Molina. "This is what love feels like."

"That our paperwork?" Darwin pointed at the black binder.

"Just in case." Gabe handed it to Anna. "We have to file

an incident report with our company for the shooting; you want that too when it's done?"

"Not so far, but I'll let you know if that changes. Excuse me one sec." She stepped away to call it in.

Darwin stood there next to Molina, Gabe and Cal across from them, nobody sure what to talk about now. Finally Molina said, "That's a loud weapon, the AK."

Darwin nodded. "Very. You get a lot of them out here?"

"Oh yeah. AKs, knockoff Bushmaster AR-15s, even a few grenade launchers."

"Goddam," Cal said, "I was just kidding about the bazooka."

Darwin said, "We think that hand grenade was South Korean."

"Seen a few of them. Stolen, black market, given to Central American governments a long ass time ago, found their way to the cartels. These guys are no joke. And shooting is a nice way to go. Couple times we've had ranchers find a body washed up, arms and legs hacked off, sometimes no head."

"A statement?" Gabe said.

"The usual. Keep your mouth shut, do what we say or else. Tell you what, I find the guys with the machetes or whatever they're using, I pray nobody else is around. These guys understand body bags, not handcuffs."

Anna came back into the group and handed the binder to Gabe. "They're checking. If you're all cleared I'll hear back in about thirty. If not, save me the hassle and just scoot over the border before I have to come back with helicopters, yeah?"

"Puerto Vallarta's nice," Cal said.

Anna looked at Darwin. "We're gonna head back to the station, get set up for tonight. Should be back here around dinner, you guys want us to bring anything? There's a helluva Tex-Mex place outside Presidio."

"Whatever's best on the menu, bring two for each of us," Darwin said, reaching for his money clip.

"Hold up," Anna said. "I'll tell Marty we're bringing it. Let's see if he offers to buy."

Gabe nodded. "Sound tactics."

"Hey, you guys are getting shot at and almost blown up so he can collect taxpayer money. Least he can do is buy you dinner."

●●●

Maro watched them through his binoculars from behind some scrub brush, sitting with his back against a rock. Darwin and the woman from Border Patrol, whose name was Anna something if he remembered right, split off and walked toward Marty's trailer.

"Let me see," Arturo said.

"They're just walking."

"Those pants, I want to see her walking away."

"You've seen enough women do that. Look, watch him walk past my tracks going to the steps, where I was right under him."

"I'd love to, but . . ."

"There he goes, didn't notice a thing. I should have left better ones, let him see how close we were to each other."

Arturo didn't say anything, just spit between his feet and watched the ground soak it up. Let him pout, Maro thought. He should have brought his binoculars. Maro watched Darwin knock on the trailer door and open it for the woman and they went inside. Maro scanned to the right, saw the other Border agent standing with the two men who had been in the front seat of the Suburban on the highway. They were just talking, nothing exciting. Marty's crewmen had gone into their middle trailer and Maro knew they wouldn't come out until the agents were gone.

Maro held the binoculars out for Arturo, who looked at them for a few seconds, then took them.

"Put them away," Maro said. "And go get a few of the boys, get them ready to bring the farmer up here. The *mujado* with the cowboy hat."

"What for?"

Maro leaned to the left and pulled his *saperka* out of its sheath, a pocket of stiff canvas that held the fixed shovel blade. He checked the tool's edge; it was sharp enough. "When your girlfriend over there leaves, I'm going to show these guys across the river something."

●●●

Darwin closed the door behind him and Anna, the air inside a little warmer this early in the day. Marty was in his chair behind the desk and Dave was on the couch, closing a leather folder with a yellow legal pad inside. Darwin told Marty, "They're shutting this whole place down."

"*What?*"

"Not really. You want some Tex-Mex?"

Anna said, "We're coming back tonight for a little stakeout."

"Fucking gave me a heart attack," Marty said. "You solve anything out there?"

"Well," Anna said, "it looks like some bad folks from the other side of the river decided to try your backyard for a night crossing. We're thinking drug run, maybe guns. We'll see tonight if they try again close by."

"Anything you need, just let me know. Pat here can put his guys wherever you need them."

"I already offered," Darwin said. "She basically told me to take a nap."

"That's what you heard?" Anna said. To Marty: "These guys are here to protect you and your site, so that's what they should do. I think you all ought to head into town and get hotel rooms for the night."

"Hey," Marty said, his finger jabbing down onto his desk, "we ain't running."

Anna's boot came over and hit the side of Darwin's, a light tap, and Darwin had to fight to keep a straight face. "Marty, I agree with her. I'd like to stick around in case anyone needs our help, but it's in our best interests to get you away from here."

"Not gonna happen. Dave, if you wanna go, that's fine. But I'm staying."

"I'll stay," Dave said from the couch.

Guy would rather face an AK than deal with Marty picking at him, Darwin thought. He said to Marty, "Understand this: If Cal or Gabe or I come in here tonight and tell you it's time to go, you go. Same for you, Dave."

"Whatever you say," Dave said.

"Give me a scenario," Marty said. "What could initiate our retreat?"

Now Anna was pushing at the side of his foot, almost moving him. "We'll beat feet if this area even looks like it's going to be overrun, if grenades start flying, if we're going to get caught in a crossfire." He shrugged. "It's a game-time decision. I can't give you a definitive list."

"Hm." He swiveled a few times, picked up a solid black construction radio from his desk. "What channel are we on?"

"I'll check," Darwin said.

"What's the codeword for retreat? How about 'Remember the Alamo?'"

Anna coughed into her fist. "Excuse me."

Darwin was right there with her but couldn't help liking Marty's idea, just a bit. "We can use that, but it'll probably sound a lot like us grabbing you by the shirt and dragging you into the Suburban."

Marty said, "Those guys come back and try to mess with my site, you're gonna *have* to drag me. And not because the shit out there costs so much—we're insured up the ass—it's the principle." He waved them away. "Look at me telling you. You guys know what I mean. Okay, so we're all on the same page. Good. Dave, give them your report on the damage to the Suburban."

Darwin and Anna turned to look at Dave, who opened the folder in his lap and flipped to a page in the legal pad. "There is no visible damage," he said, and looked up to field any questions.

Anna nodded, kept a straight face for Darwin as she turned back to Marty, and said, "If you find anything, just let us know. We're bringing Darwin and his guys some food from Oasis; would you like anything?"

Marty put both hands flat on his desk, holding it down. "Oh lord, pork tacos. Dave, grab the take-out menu from the kitchen and let the guys order some dinner. And give Agent Ricks some cash, make sure it covers everybody." He winked at Darwin. "We'll have a nice picnic, case the world ends tonight."

●●●

Darwin walked with Anna and Molina to their truck and watched her get into the driver's seat. Cal and Gabe were walking up the hill behind him.

"Those two are gonna follow you out," he said to Anna. "We need some supplies from town, and I guess I should tell you, they include additional firearms."

"I saw in the paperwork you guys are licensed for more than the side arms you're carrying. Anything coming out here that wasn't in the file?"

"No ma'am," Darwin said.

"Are any of these weapons equipped with a scope? Some kind of aiming device?"

Darwin gave her the corner of his eye. "Some."

"That's good. Maybe next time you shoot, you'll actually hit something. See ya tonight."

She rolled out and Darwin stood in the low dust from her tires and tried to think of a comeback. Then what, chase after the truck until she stops? Run up to the window and she rolls it down, says, "This better be good."

"Look at that grin," Cal said. He tossed his go bag into the Suburban and shook his head at Darwin. "Married guys, shit. Both of ya, drooling and fumbling around."

Gabe froze halfway through the driver's door. "The hell you talking about? All I did was bring her the files. Figured I did any more, Sheepdog would stab me in the face."

"All right," Darwin said.

Cal said, "You're both lucky she's too skinny for me." He gave it some thought. "But twist my arm, get me a bottle of Jack. I could close my eyes and take one for the team."

"I'll let her know," Darwin said.

"You know Christine can sense this kind of shit," Cal said. "Right now she's looking into her cauldron, chewing on eye of newt and planning your demise."

Darwin watched the Border Patrol truck get smaller on the two-track that twisted out to the highway. There was tall brush out there that would hide it for a few seconds at a time. "She got the divorce papers."

"You're kidding," Cal said.

"Nah. Wants me to come home and sign them."

Cal looked at Gabe, came back to Darwin and spread his arms, closing in. "Congratulations, brother. Welcome back to happiness." He wrapped Darwin in a bear hug, picked him up and shook him.

When he was back on the ground Darwin said, "Am I supposed to be happy?"

"Fuck yeah you are. She makes you miserable."

Gabe shrugged. "I'd be tore up if Shelly left me. But she don't enjoy ripping balls off like Christine does, so . . ."

"Man, you're better off," Cal said. "After this job we'll go sign the papers, then you and me'll hit it hard. Lock and load, seek and destroy, all sluts and skanks beware."

Gabe said, "I think he'd rather spend some time in Border Agent Ricks' cell."

"I love therapy," Darwin said.

"Oh hey," Cal said. He reached over and rubbed Darwin's stomach. "You still got room for pancakes with all those love butterflies in your tum-tum?"

"Gabe, will you run him over three or four times?"

CHAPTER 10

DARWIN HAD HIS lawn chair in the spot on the hill, the sun on the back of his neck and working toward the top of his head. He had his coat off and the binoculars in his lap. He felt good, knowing something close to an operation was planned that night. He ran it through his head, kept coming to a scene where he checked on Anna and Molina, found just her, Molina off somewhere taking a leak.

Well, hello.

Hello back.

Daring him to make a move.

Be a professional, he thought. Remember the whole AK-47/grenade thing?

He came back, saw Jim and another crewman, Brad maybe, over at the tower site. Looking at prints and pointing. The Conex down there was open, the doors on the far side so he couldn't see in. He didn't know where the other two engineers were. He took a drink from a bottle of water and saw movement in the hills across the river and his first thought was: Amateurs, moving around like that.

Then: No, I'm supposed to see this.

He brought the binoculars up and saw the guy from the Jeep and the shootout, *Lobo*, waving at him. Darwin wished he had something else to call him. He was looking back with his own set of binoculars and he stopped waving and held his hand out, Stop, then made an OK with his thumb and forefinger.

Darwin frowned behind his binoculars. What the hell is this? Was he calling for a cease-fire? The guy was waiting for something, so Darwin gave him an OK back. *Lobo* said something and another guy, tan and lean and younger, came up from behind a rock and took the binoculars, stepped out of the way so two other men—stocky and dark, these guys Mexican for sure—could drag an older man up to *Lobo*. The old man had a cowboy hat on and *Lobo* pointed at it, then across the river to Darwin's left, toward the gulley.

"Wait a minute," Darwin said to his binoculars. Cowboy hat—he'd said something about it last night, asking *Lobo* if he was wearing one. Telling him he'd seen a cowboy hat in the darkness, and now here's this poor old guy with the hat.

"No, come on," Darwin said. He watched *Lobo* hold something up and recognized it right away, a *saperka*, the straight-blade entrenching shovel like the Russians carried.

"No, don't you do it."

The old man struggled but couldn't keep his arm from getting pulled out straight. *Lobo* looked at Darwin, no binoculars but his face saying: I know you're watching. He swung the shovel down with two hands and got halfway through the old man's elbow joint. He pulled it out and hit the spot again and got through, the lower arm coming away in the stocky guy's hands.

The old man looked at his arm and couldn't believe the blood coming out of it, falling onto the rock at his feet. His neck clenched up and a few seconds later Darwin heard the scream roll up the hill, quiet but no way to mistake what it was. Darwin stood up and pulled the .45 and pointed it at the hill across the river, ridiculous at a mile away, but he couldn't help it.

He turned away from the binoculars and looked down at Jim and Brad. They hadn't heard the scream, still standing around doing nothing.

"God*dam* it."

Through the binoculars he saw the other lean one watching him. He said something to *Lobo*, who waved at Darwin to welcome him back then swung the shovel into the old man's shoulder and had to hack at it again and again to get through. The old man was still screaming, looking at his arm getting chopped off, not even blinking while the blood splashed onto his face and his cowboy hat.

Darwin took a step. Even with his knees he could run a sub-six mile when he had to. He could get across the river and up the hill in what, ten minutes, tops, if he didn't get swept downstream. The old man might bleed out by then but he might not. Either way he could kill everyone else.

Get real. At least four guys holding the high ground, three AR-15s and one AK leaning against the rock right there. You'd die before the old man, wait for him at the Pearlies and say, Hey, I tried.

Oh yeah, and it's fucking Mexico over there.

He put the .45 back and squeezed the binoculars with both hands. The old man was fading, about to pass out. *Lobo* stepped back from him and took a stance like a batter. The two stocky guys ducked down but kept the old man up and *Lobo* looked over at Darwin and smiled, stepped forward and hit the man in the neck, again, getting through it all until there was just a flap of skin and the old man's head tipped back and his body sagged.

"You motherfucker," Darwin said.

Lobo held his arms up in victory, then stuck the shovel into the dirt. He reached down and pulled the old man's head the rest of the way off, let it drop but kept the cowboy hat. He put it on and tipped it to Darwin, looked around at his men and got nods of approval. Then he yanked it off and sniffed the inside, made a face and sailed the hat down the hill like a Frisbee.

He took a deep breath and patted his stomach: What to

do now? He acted surprised to see the binoculars being handed to him, took them and checked to see what Darwin had to say about it all.

"You see me?" Darwin said. "Good."

He brought the binoculars down and flicked a thumb across his throat.

He made his lips easy to read: "I. Will. Kill. You."

Then he sat back down and didn't bother with the binoculars because it didn't matter what they thought of it.

●●●

Darwin called Gabe and Cal and told them about it. He finished with, "These guys are telling us they aren't fucking around. So be ready for anything on the road."

"Haven't seen a thing so far," Cal said. "Be nice if they wait 'til we pick up the crates. Give 'em the good news with a little full auto."

"Keep me posted, I'll do likewise."

Darwin called Hank next, about seven o'clock in Baghdad, and gave him the details. "I'll tell Border about it, but I don't know what they can do."

"Nothing," Hank said. "But at least they'll know the guy with the shovel's an asshole."

"I'm this close to pulling Marty and his guys out of here right now."

There was a delay, but it wasn't the connection. Phalanx didn't skimp on comms. "Are they in immediate danger?"

"What's immediate? I got a crew with bad intentions about a mile away as we speak, last night they were inside a hundred yards. Tonight could be the same deal."

"Hey," Hank said, "over here you had guys in the next car woulda blown you up if they'd known you were behind the tinted windows. Our contract is to protect the personnel and assets. Wherever they are. Marty wants to pitch a tent in a live volcano, we gotta keep him from getting burned."

"Please don't say that to him," Darwin said.

"I'm working on getting more guys your way, but everybody's booked up. If I can get some new hires up and running, you want 'em?"

"Send their files first. I'll let you know."

"Will do. Hey, why is Christine calling the office trying to get your location?"

"You're shitting me."

"No sir. Couple times a day, trying to wear us down. Says she has something for you."

"Yeah, divorce papers."

Another delay. "Well," Hank said, "there is a God. You want her to send them to the office?"

"No, I don't want them."

"Why not?"

"Hank, I got enough shit to worry about right now."

"Sign the papers, that's a huge pile of shit you don't have to deal with ever again. That came out wrong—I'm not calling your wife a huge pile of shit. I'm saying she *gives* you a huge pile of shit."

"I'll tell her to stop calling the office."

"Whatever we can do, just let me know. And you're sending the incident reports?"

"Sometime today."

"Good stuff. Hey Patrick?"

"Yeah."

"Don't cause any international incidents."

"Copy."

"And I love you."

Darwin shook his head, couldn't help grinning. "Great. Bye."

●●●

Darwin watched Jim and possibly Brad work at the tower site for an hour, no movement across the Rio except the cowboy hat blowing around the hill until it fell into the water and was gone.

He got his phone out and scrolled to Christine, rubbed his thumb over the Call button. Not to tell her about the farmer—he never told her the things he saw and did—but just hear her voice.

Hear it say what?

You ready to sign the papers yet?

Darwin put the phone away and scowled at the hills across the river, willing the bastards over there to walk across and face him again. Come on. Dave came out of Marty's trailer and waved, came up the slope with an aluminum carafe of coffee.

"Refill?"

Darwin popped the top off his travel mug. "Thanks much. How's Marty doing?"

"He's concerned," Dave said.

"I told him we can pack up and hit a hotel. Soon as he's ready."

"No, not that," Dave said. He looked for a place to sit down, hiked up his slacks instead and squatted next to the lawn chair. "Thing is, it's in your contract not to divulge any industry information you come across while you're on the job here."

Darwin sipped his coffee.

Dave said, "But law enforcement, Border Patrol in this case, has no such clause."

"Marty's worried about trade secrets?"

"It's plausible that another company, a competitor, could offer them compensation for any information about what we're doing here and how we're doing it. Or worse, certain organizations across the border could bribe or coerce for the same information."

Darwin scanned the hills over there. It was a decent point. "We can't tell Border to stay away. This is government land."

"I understand," Dave said. "But if at all possible, we'd like to keep unauthorized personnel out of the trailers and away from the tower site."

"Would you like me to pass that along to the agents?"

"Oh no, we don't want to be rude about it. But if you could discourage any sort of loitering, snooping around, that kind of thing."

"Discourage."

"Please. It's my understanding they don't expect the troublemakers from last night to come through the same spot again, so it may not be an issue."

"Let's hope," Darwin said. "I wouldn't want to be rude."

Dave reached out and touched his knee. "I know you're in a tough spot, and I apologize. But we're all here to get a job done, right?"

"Right on, Dale Carnegie." The look on Dave's face made Darwin smile. "Army didn't just train me to shoot."

Dave recovered. "We appreciate your cooperation on this."

"Hm. You know where the other two engineers are? Eric and John, if I recall."

"Ah, not for sure." Dave stood up, wiped off dirt that wasn't there. "I think they drove to the next site to collect some measurements."

"In what? The pickups are here."

"Do you need to talk to them?"

Darwin looked at him, something in the tone. "No. Just want to know where everybody is, make sure they're safe."

"Let me get them on the radio, check on their location and status."

"Maybe I can get one of those to hold onto."

"Sure," Dave said. "Now, or do you want to pick it up later?"

"Later's fine. Just shoot me a thumbs-up when you get in touch with them."

"Absolutely."

Dave took the carafe back down the hill. Darwin watched him go, thinking: What the hell is going on out here?

●●●

Darwin was in the middle trailer looking for lunch when the four engineers walked in. The trailer was partitioned off about halfway along its length, the bigger front space a kitchen and sitting area with a door to the back room that had cots, six of them crammed close together, and the bathroom at the back. All the engineers were sweaty and dusty, but Eric and John were covered in wet dirt, a different color and scent than what Darwin and the others had on their boots.

"You two find a pig to wrestle?" Darwin said.

Eric laughed, said, "Had to dig another damn hole at the next site, get a rock sample in for testing."

"You walked?"

Eric looked at John, a quick glance, then back into the refrigerator, choosing a soda. "Yeah, faster to do that as the crow flies than to take the truck around on the two-track."

John didn't say anything. Eric got his soda and sat down, tapped the top and cracked it open. Jim pulled a box of beef patties out of the freezer.

"Grilling up some burgers for lunch, how many can I put on for you?"

"Two would be great, if you can spare 'em," Darwin said. He didn't smell the booze on Jim anymore. Sweated it all out.

"Medium rare okay? I refuse to burn the taste out."

"Works for me." Darwin filled his water bottle from the cooler next to the fridge. "Hey, I see you got an extra bunk in there. We have a snorer in our midst, so if you wake up and find a guy bound and gagged in there, don't panic."

Jim barked a laugh. Everybody else at the table had a tight smile or a blank face.

Got it, no more snoring jokes, Darwin thought. The energy in the trailer was pulled tight, the only sound the bubbles gurgling to the top of the inverted water bottle.

After ten seconds Brad said, "Man, that was intense this morning. We could get more of the same tonight?"

Darwin put the top on his water, set the bottle on the table. "All right guys. I'm gonna lay it out for you. I don't know what Marty told you is the priority right now, far as timelines and industry secrets, but goal number one is keeping everybody safe. You can finish this job a month or a year from now, long as you're still alive."

He looked them over. Jim had his hand on the doorknob, the box of patties in the other hand like a waiter's tray.

"You start doing stupid stuff, wandering off to dig holes or whatever without security, and you get snatched or shot, your last thought will probably be, Man, that really wasn't worth it."

"We've been doing it every day so far," Jim said. "Not stupid stuff, just . . . working."

"That was pre-engagement. We are now post-engagement. Adaptation is necessary. Maybe Marty told you not to let us limit your productivity, maybe you had to take care of some shit before Border shows up. I don't care. I'm going next door to get a radio, and from now on I want status updates every hour. You check in, tell me where you are. That's until my guys get back, then we'll have overwatch on everybody, all the time."

Jim checked the guys at the table, came back to Darwin. "This is okay with Marty?"

"Doesn't have to be. What I'm asking for doesn't impede your ability to do your job." He scanned the faces. "Does it?"

Nobody said anything.

Darwin reached back and knocked on the wood paneling. "This isn't bullet resistant. Hell, I'd call it a bullet *mag*net. Pure dumb luck that an AK round didn't zip through here last night and catch one of you. I highly recommend you go into town tonight. One of my guys will go with you, low profile. You can watch ESPN, go to a titty bar, whatever."

They all looked at each other, the table, the door. Jim put the box of patties on the table, said, "I need to get Marty up to speed on some other things. I can run this past him, see what he says." He opened the door.

Darwin said, "You want me to come along? Might be better coming from me."

"Nah, I got it. I'll bring you a radio." He stepped out and closed the door and the trailer was silent.

Darwin stood with a nice little smile and waited to see if it would work, but nobody talked. He wasn't ready to corner them yet, go aggro, so he told the guys to be safe and he'd swing by to pick up his burgers when they were done. He walked out and wandered up to his lawn chair, the trailers behind him feeling like a couple of beehives.

●●●

The sun was dropping when Cal called and said they were twenty minutes out, all cargo—including cold pancakes—on board and no trouble coming or going, except the gun store owner who gave them the stink eye about the 5.56mm ammo until they showed him credentials. Then he invited them over for smoked brisket.

"So you owe me some Texas brisket," Cal said. "Broke my

heart, telling him no."

Darwin was hungry again, the paper plate from the burgers under his chair with the empty Pepsi can and construction radio holding it down. John had brought it all up to him, made worthless small talk and gone back into the middle trailer as soon as he could. Now the four engineers were milling around the tower site doing things that didn't look like work, but could be if you had the right degree.

Hold the pancakes for breakfast tomorrow, Darwin thought. Save your appetite for Anna's Tex-Mex. He heard the Suburban coming. He stood, popped his knees and back, and met Cal and Gabe in the parking area. Cal handed him a plastic bag with a hard plastic container inside.

"Don't trust the sausage."

Darwin saw the M4A1 across Cal's lap, hanging from the three-point sling, and the Benelli M4 Super 90 wedged between Gabe's seat and the middle console. Cal's assault rifle had the SOPMOD accessory kit—rail interface system, vertical foregrip, Trijicon Reflex sight, Streamlight LED flashlight, and Gemtech TREK suppressor—everything but the detachable M203 grenade launcher, which was a no-no in most countries and a pain in the ass to get ammo for. Gabe's shotgun had an Aimpoint Micro sight along with the Streamlight. Darwin smelled the gun oil, happy the right tools were on-site.

"Anything going on across the water?" Gabe said.

"Nada. Either they wore themselves out murdering that guy or they're getting ready for something tonight."

Cal said, "Want me to go for a little swim? I promise to be home before Border shows up."

"Yeah, soaking wet and out of breath, you look at the agents, say, What?"

Cal just raised his eyebrows behind his sunglasses, waiting. Darwin had already run through it from his lawn chair, the pros and cons.

"Not yet," he said.

•••

The three hard plastic Pelican shipping crates were different sizes, one tall and square, one trunk-sized, and one long and flat. Darwin and Gabe stacked the trunk and square one carried them to the lawn chair. Cal followed with the long one, careful to keep it from bumping against his leg.

At the chair they popped the locks on the trunk and square crates and Cal rooted through, got his MICH helmet, five spare magazines and a night spotting scope. He closed and stacked them for Darwin and Gabe to carry the rest of the way down.

"Hurry up and no grunting," he said. The long flat crate stayed with him.

Gabe walked backward down the slope and took most of the weight. The engineers watched from the tower site, and Darwin wondered if they were happy about the added firepower. Didn't look like it.

Marty and Dave were waiting at the steps to the trailer, Marty with a tumbler of something swirling in one hand. "What did we get?"

"Rest of the gear," Darwin said.

"Well let's have a look."

Gabe looked at Darwin—Keep going?—but Darwin set his end down and Gabe did the same. Darwin set the square case in front of Marty while Gabe popped the latches on the trunk.

"Just got a call from Agent Anna," Marty said. He put his foot on the square case and leaned on his knee. "They're about an hour away, four of 'em this time. Hey, Agent Anna—that sounds like something we'd use to kill gooks in 'Nam. Or no, now we're using it to kill wetbacks in Texas." He looked at

Dave and got a nod.

Darwin kept his eyes on the crates so he wouldn't punch Marty in the throat. Gabe removed the trunk's top.

"Hello," Marty said.

The crate could hold six assault rifles but now only had Darwin's shorty M4 and Gabe's AR-15 A3 Tactical, both with the Trijicon ACOG 4x32 sight, Streamlight, and slings. The Gemtech suppressors for the long guns and pistols were underneath in their transit pouches. The rest of the space in the crate, besides the two empty slots for Cal's M4 and the shotgun, was packed with night optics, extra mags for everything and the shitty ammunition they'd brought from Baghdad.

Marty turned toward the Rio and yelled, "Try it now, assholes." He took a sip and nodded at the guns. "This is good. I feel good. Hey, Jim came by earlier, said you told the guys to pack it in tonight."

"I told them safety is primary, and it would be safer to not be here tonight. Same thing I told you."

"Pat, we gotta have a united front for the troops. They see us divided, or panicking, and all hell breaks loose."

Gabe was kneeling with his back to Marty, putting the crate lid on. He rested a hand on the AR-15, looked at Darwin for the green light.

Darwin crossed his arms and said, "Okay Marty, what is the united front? I get the feeling we're basing our recommendations on incomplete intel here."

"Incomplete?" Marty said.

"You familiar with the phrase 'information asymmetry'?"

Marty swirled his glass. "You think I'm hiding something?"

"I think you aren't telling us everything we need to know to keep you and your crew as safe as possible."

That hung between them. Gabe got out from underneath it and stood next to Darwin.

"Well you're wrong," Marty said. "By definition—shit, by

law according to the contract you signed—what you need to know is *exactly* what I tell you. And what I'm telling you right now is don't talk to my guys any more, other than the radio updates. You have any questions or requests, come to me or Dave. Clear on that? Have we achieved information symmetry?"

Darwin took a deep breath. Gabe took a small step that would let him get between Darwin and Marty if he had to. Marty looked into his tumbler, tossed what was left into the dirt and handed the glass to Dave.

"Look, I don't want to be a dick," he said, "but I'm dealing with deadlines and up-the-ass government oversight on top of all this happy horseshit." He waved at the hills across the Rio. "What I need from you is confidence that you can handle the latter so I can stop worrying about it."

"We can handle it," Darwin said.

"Good. Settled. When Agent Anna gets here, I want you and her outside my trailer for a meeting. It won't take long." Marty walked away, around the corner to his trailer. Dave stayed a beat longer and stared at the ground with his lips pursed, hands behind his back, then he followed.

Gabe said, "How you doing Sheepdog?"

"Hey, same shit, different client. But if we have to drag his ass into the truck, I'm taking the long way."

CHAPTER 11

DARWIN TOOK A walk up the hill and along the two-track to meet the Border Patrol a quarter mile from the parking area as the sun was disappearing. He was in full kit: armor, helmet, radio with earpiece and throat mic, pouches with extra magazines for the M4 and the .45.

He'd swapped the ACOG sight for his DBAL-I[2] with the green infrared laser pointer and infrared illumination for his night optics, resting in a belt pouch now but could clip onto the front of his helmet and snug up to his face. He wanted his eyes to get used to the darkness, wouldn't use the night optics unless he had to. It was nice to wear it all without losing ten pounds of sweat, though most of it still smelled like Baghdad.

The agents rolled up in two trucks, lights off, Anna driving the lead vehicle with Molina next to her. She had her window down and Darwin could smell the Tex-Mex.

"Hey, you—good hell, that smells delicious."

"Get your head out of my window." She eyed the M4 hanging on the sling across Darwin's chest, the suppressor attached now, all the other gear hanging off it. "Can that thing make me a latté?"

"Decaf okay?"

She made a face, turned to Molina. "This could be a hijacking; protect the Tex-Mex."

Darwin stepped back, his stomach growling. "You might want to leave the trucks here. Me and a guy across the river were watching each other earlier, so they have eyes on the parking area."

"What did he look like?"

"An asshole."

"Do they have night optics?"

"Not that I saw, but we can stay hidden down to the trailers. Marty wants to chat with you and me before you settle in. Tell us all to be careful out there."

"Great."

He waited while she parked and the second truck did a K-turn to face the other way so they had a truck ready to go either direction. The two agents got out and Darwin shook hands with them, Agents Nuñez and Foster, Nuñez short and beefy, Foster short and lean. They both checked the M4 but didn't say anything.

Molina and Foster dropped the tailgates on both trucks and got their gear going. Anna handed Darwin a heavy, open-top cardboard box, the smells coming out of it enough to buckle his knees. She grabbed another box the same size and they headed down the two-track.

She was bundled up for the night: gloves, a thick coat over her body armor, a dark scarf around her neck and a knit watch cap. The only word Darwin could think of to describe her was adorable.

Yeah, he thought. Say that word and see how fast she can go hot with that AR she's toting.

He looked back at the trucks to make sure they were far enough and said, "I'll leave it up to you to tell your team, but the guy across the river murdered someone today. Broad daylight."

She stopped for a moment, looking at him, then walked again, slower. "Across the border?"

"Yeah, in the hills over there. Agent Molina mentioned something this morning about you guys finding bodies chopped up along the river. This could be your guy."

"You watched him do that? Who was the victim?"

"Some poor guy. And it was my fault." He told her about the old guy in the cowboy hat and the *saperka*.

"God, those poor people," she said. "I guarantee you this fucker had something over the victim. His family, his farm, who knows. But that old guy didn't want to be here. And the assailant, he wants you to call him *Lobo*?"

"Pretty much."

"What a douche. You can't pick your own nickname."

They were in the tall scrub along the parking area about to go downhill. "Hold that thought," Darwin said, and turned them on an angle toward Cal in the lawn chair.

• • •

"Here's the deal," Cal said, his Styrofoam container of pork tacos and enchiladas open in his lap. Darwin was glad it was dark and he wouldn't have to see the beard aftermath. He and Anna were hunkered down in the brush a few feet from the chair, trying to stay hidden even though Cal had been scanning the hills across the border with the 7X night scope and didn't see anybody. Gabe had switched off the breaker to the site's single floodlight to preserve the night optics advantage, if there was one.

Cal said, "I tried to defy the Laws of Nicknames a few years ago. The Gods allowed me to live as an example to others."

Anna looked at Darwin. He nodded.

Cal said, "My last name is Wafer. Guess which nickname-slash-call sign got stamped on my forehead the first day of basic."

"Nilla," Anna said.

"You are correct. Now I knew better than to question the wisdom of my superior officers, but once I got out and became a contractor, I figured, hey, I'm a free man. I'll decide what you call me. So I'm on the job in Iraq, the beard's looking good, I'm bulletproof, and I decide my new call sign will be Infidel."

"No," Anna said.

"Oh, I'm afraid so Anna. I put the word out and it lasted a good four minutes before guys started calling me Fidel. Ten minutes after that I was Castro. Then some literate bastard jumped in and changed it to Castrato. Know what that means?"

"It doesn't sound good."

"No, no it doesn't. Why don't you ask the gentleman next to you, since he's the one who came up with it?"

Anna turned to Darwin.

"It's a male with a soprano singing voice. Caused by a condition that keeps him from maturing sexually, or by castration before puberty."

Anna put a glove to her mouth.

"Yeah," Cal said. "So I had a new call sign for about twenty minutes, then I had to buy three bottles of whiskey to get a houseful of assholes to call me Nilla again. What's your call sign?"

"Molina and I are Marfa-One, our sector and team number, but sometimes they call me Rickshaw. Because of Ricks."

Cal considered it. "Okay, not great, but not horrible. Embrace it and don't look back."

"Thanks Nilla."

"Any time. Thanks for the grub."

Darwin said, "I told her about what happened across the river."

Cal looked at Anna. "Anything you guys can do about it?"

"Pass it up the chain, let authorities on the Mike side

know about it. Other than that . . ."

Cal nodded, took a huge bite of taco and said, "Fido."

"What?"

Darwin nudged her. "He's eating. We're invisible for the next fifteen minutes."

They picked up the boxes and threaded through the brush down toward the trailers. Darwin waited for an opening that would let them walk next to each other.

"He said Fido. Stands for Fuck It, Drive On. I'm sure you have it happen, you see some things go down you'd very much like to prevent, but your hands are tied by laws, bureaucracy, orders, whatever. Running ops, we'd be places we weren't supposed to be, seeing shit we weren't supposed to see, and nobody wanted to hear it anyway. It happens enough, and you let it get to you, you're done. So fuck it, drive on."

"Wish I'd heard that a few years ago. Does it help?"

"Not really."

They walked down the hill in darkness. The scenario popped into Darwin's head, where he came across Anna on the stakeout, just the two of them. He cleared his throat, thought: Is she waiting for me to try something? Am I out of my fucking mind?

She said, "Is Marty still talking Alamo, last stand and all that?"

"Oh yeah. I tried to get his crew to head into town for the night and he jumped up my ass. Probably still in a hissy, so be ready."

Darwin wanted to tell her how everybody on site was acting squirrelly, holding back about something. But Dave had reminded him earlier, underneath the buddy-buddy bullshit about everyone trying to get a job done: Your contract prohibits you from discussing client issues with outside parties.

Darwin walked with Anna and kept his mouth shut.

Fido.

●●●

Darwin left Anna on the back side of Marty's trailer and carried the boxes inside, set them on the table with all the engineers and Dave sitting in silence while Marty worked his way out from behind his desk. Darwin looked at the beer bottles on the table and the whiskey in front of Jim, who was staring at the M4. He glanced up to Darwin's face and pulled the bottle closer but didn't open it. His glass had a half-inch left at the bottom.

Marty stepped outside.

"Around back," Darwin told him, then looked at the engineers. "Stay sharp, guys," he said, and closed the door.

Marty sang on his way around the corner. "Oh, Agent Anna, oh don't you cry for me . . . Hey, thanks for bringing the food. You have enough money?"

"Got your change right here," Anna said.

"Keep it, get some breakfast tomorrow morning."

Anna pressed the bills against his chest. "Take it."

"Suit yourself." Marty folded them into his pocket. "Okay, the way I see it, my team is better off in one spot so you don't have to worry about protecting two structures. Am I right?"

"With the manpower we have, yes," Darwin said. "But it also makes one target for anybody coming across the border. How do you feel about spending the night in the Conex?"

"You're serious?"

"It's pretty much an armored car."

Anna looked at the big steel box with the pickups parked next to it. She nodded.

"There's a lot of crap in there," Marty said.

Darwin said, "Knowing the guys across the river have eyes on us, I didn't want to move you in while the sun was up.

This one is my first choice. What's in the other one, down by —"

"Even more crap," Marty said. "Listen, I think everyone would like to avoid getting locked in a steel crate, if at all possible."

"Spread the word. Things get hairy, option A is the Suburban. Option B is the shipper. Any way I can get the keys?"

"They have different locks, so just the keys for this one?"

"How about you unlock it now," Darwin said, "and keep the other set handy."

Marty looked at the shipper, rubbed his neck and scanned the darkness toward the Rio. "Where are you guys going to be? Anna?"

"Right now the plan is to set up with one team on the far side of the gulley and string out from there. We'll have to see what the landscape dictates."

"Good, okay. Pat?"

Darwin rested his hands on the M4. "We have overwatch from the hillside, probably keep one of us static near the trailer and one guy as a rover." He looked at Anna. "We'll stay out of your sector, so no worries about friendly fire."

"The way you shoot? Who's worried?"

"Super. As I was saying, because I'm a professional, I'll let you know if we need to come your way and I'd appreciate it if you'd do the same."

"Can do."

"Marty, I need you to black out the windows or keep the lights off."

"All of them?"

"Bright windows are a sniper's best friend. And they'll silhouette us walking around out here."

"All of them, yes or no?"

"Yes please," Darwin said. He drummed his fingers on the stock and upper receiver.

Marty turned so he could examine the trailer. "I guess."

He faced Anna. "Well, I'll let you get set up. You want to leave a radio with me?"

"I have your cell number," she said.

"I'll keep it close. Pat, you can use your phone or the radio I let you borrow. We have one on my desk in there. Okay, I'm gonna go eat and get everybody started on our little arts and crafts project."

He walked away counting the windows out loud. There were two on this side, plus the door.

Anna waited until he was inside. "You wanna kick something, I won't judge you."

"Nah, I'm good. Long as I know he's the asshole in the relationship, I can plan accordingly."

She cocked her head. "I can't see you being an asshole."

Tell her you're married, Darwin thought. He said, "That's because so far our goals are aligned. They diverge, you'll see I can be a tremendous asshole. We should swap numbers too, case the radios take a break."

He didn't think of it as getting her number until they both had their phones out, heads bowed while they punched buttons.

He said, "I call this number, it isn't going to be some asshole hotline or anything."

"Try it now."

"I trust you. Give my number to your crew, let 'em know I'll have my phone on at all times." Cover it up with at least a little business.

"Hm. Enjoy your dinner."

"Thanks." He tapped the radio on his vest. "We're on frequency twenty-two."

"Fourteen," she said. "How much is it worth to keep your channel from Marty?"

"Are you shaking me down? I got five whole dollars on me right now."

"Who said it has to be cash?"

Something bobbed in Darwin's stomach. "Well–"

"Maybe I can put a few downrange with that sports car you call a rifle."

"Deal," he said. Christ, get it together. "Let me know when you're in place, we'll get your locations fixed."

"Sounds good."

They stood there and looked at each other until she clapped her gloves and turned and walked up the hill. Darwin's earpiece clicked. He pressed the throat mic.

"Go ahead."

Cal said, "Why didn't you kiss her?"

Darwin sent a squelch back. Fucking night vision.

●●●

Marty closed the trailer door and slapped the light switches down.

"Hey," Jim said.

Marty heard a bottle clink against a glass. "We're under orders, no lights. So unless you wanna cover all the windows, we get to sit here in the dark." He felt his way along the wall and ran his left thigh into the corner of his desk.

"Godammit." He found his chair and dropped into it. "Wait, turn the lights back on."

They came on and Dave kept his finger on the switch, watched Marty for a few seconds. "What's up, boss?"

"Not now." Marty slid the construction radio to the left edge of his blotter, put his personal cell in the middle, then opened a desk drawer and pulled out a cheap cell phone. He put that on the far right.

Everybody was staring at the cheap phone. Marty laid his fingers on it and his cell, switched them around like three-card Monte, then did his cell and the radio.

"Ho," he said, and switched the cheap phone and the

radio. "Whup."

The engineers stared at him and the cheap phone. Dave smoothed his tie.

Marty cleared his throat and reset the original arrangement. Jesus, don't mix them up if you have to call somebody. He nodded at Dave and the trailer went black again.

Chairs creaked and bottles moved on the table.

Jim said, "You gonna call him?" His voice sounded closer in the dark.

"And what, leave a message?" Marty said. "He doesn't turn his on except to call me, then he turns it off."

"So . . ."

"So we wait, Jim."

"Shouldn't we warn him about what's going on, tell him to stay away?"

"You think he doesn't know?" Marty said. He heard whispering. "Hey, who's that? Speak up."

Jim said, "If he calls, you gonna ask about Robbie?"

"Ask him what?"

"Uh, how he's doing?"

"Uh, he's doing fine, Jim."

"How do you know?"

"Because we have a deal," Marty said.

"A deal with a mercenary hired by a drug cartel. Yeah, pretty solid."

Marty rubbed his temples. These guys just didn't get it.

Dave said, "Jim, what we—"

"Fuck you Dave." A glass thumped onto the table. "Are we seriously just going with business as usual? Darwin said we're all getting protection from now on, so how are we gonna work?"

"We'll figure it out," Marty said.

"What about when they get more guys on site? Sooner or later somebody's gonna ask to see what's in the shipper down there. I about shit myself when Darwin and the guy with the beard were gonna stand behind it when they blew that grenade."

"Cal," Dave said.

"What? Yeah, Cal, whatever. Then the fucking *Border Patrol* shows up?"

Marty said, "Okay, so I don't report it, and they find out from somebody else we got automatic gunfire and grenades going off. Guess what? Instead of two of them stopping by to chat, we get a battalion wondering what we're trying to hide."

"Maybe that wouldn't be so bad."

The trailer was silent until Marty said, "Jim, are you speaking for everyone in the crew, or just yourself?"

"I believe I speak for everyone at this table when I say I'm scared out of my fucking mind and worried sick about Robbie. Agreed?"

John, Brad, and Eric mumbled and creaked their chairs.

Dave said, "We're all very concerned."

"Motion fucking carried," Jim said. It sounded like he took a drink to celebrate.

"So you all want to go home," Marty said.

Jim snorted. "Hell yes. But what about Robbie?"

"Hey, we drop our end of the deal, you know what happens."

"Well, then we can't go home."

"So what the hell are we talking about, Jim?" Marty heard him flop around in his chair. "Nothing, that's what. Now Maro is seeing about speeding things up on his side. What can we do over here? Can we get it done before the extra security shows up?"

Jim let out a long breath. "If—"

The cheap cell phone lit up and buzzed.

•••

Maro was on the Mexican bank of the Rio, hidden in the thick brush with six of his *salvajes*, everybody squatting and leaning on their assault rifles. Marty answered during the second ring.

"Hello."

"*Hola hola*," Maro said. "It looks like you having a party over there."

"Listen, there's nothing I can do. They're setting up at the gulley and downriver in case you try to bring anything across tonight."

"No, not tonight," Maro said.

"Okay, good."

"Tonight I'm just bringing me across, with some friends. No product."

"Wait," Marty said. "I've got the security detail over here —fully armed now, by the way—plus four Border agents on a stakeout."

"Yes, I know. They brought food too, you have any left?"

"You're not listening. If there's an incident tonight, we'll have more agents, possibly Homeland, DEA, ICE, the whole fucking alphabet soup sniffing around. We'll have to stop work completely, man. There's no way we'll finish on time."

Maro said, "Oh, that's the old plan. I have a new one."

He ended the call and turned the phone off.

•••

Maro had been thinking about the new plan since the second day of the old one, the cartel's plan. On the third day he'd said to Arturo, "Man, I'm bored."

Arturo had looked at the bloody *saperka* in Maro's hands, the woman's body at his feet. "Really?"

Maro kicked the body into the Rio and rinsed his hands and the shovel, dried it and put it away. They sat on the rocks and watched the brown water slide past.

"It's because we're soldiers, not babysitters," Maro said. "Here we just make sure everyone does their job and nobody messes with them. Move something from here to there. And we put up with shit from a lazy white guy."

"Sounds like what we did for the Russians."

"Yes, but then the job was to kill Afghans. Now it's what, moving dirt? We need another war, my friend."

Arturo rubbed at a spot of fresh blood on his boot. "We're in the war against drugs."

"You're funny. Do these hills remind you of Afghanistan?"

Arturo looked around. "Maybe a little. Here though, I'm not afraid an old woman is going to sneak up while I'm sleeping and cut off my *juevos*. And there's no snow."

"Picture this," Maro said. "The land across this river becomes the staging point for an American invasion. The Mexican soldiers either welcome them or surrender and go into hiding, because, come on. The U.S. comes across and massacres any resistance from the cartels in one day. Anyone says different, show them footage of the invasion of Iraq. Yes, the cartels employ some ex-Special Forces, but they're leading thugs. The U.S. would have full teams in place, targeting houses, kicking doors in and clearing city blocks. You think some of them aren't here already, just in case?"

"You've put a lot of thought into this," Arturo said.

"Listen. The cartels fall back to Mexico City, then to the border with Guatemala. Maybe some of the old Sandinistas join in, maybe some boys from Colombia, Venezuela, if they can get north of the canal. Then what?"

Arturo thought about it. "Mexico becomes South Texas."

"Maybe someday. But for a long time the U.S. will be occupiers, and many people from here and other countries will want them out. They'll pay a lot of money to hire people who know how to fight in the hills, mountains, desert, against a brutal enemy. Not sit on a hill and make sure there are enough shovels."

"We get paid a lot to do this," Arturo said.

"Okay. I offer you right now, one million dollars to cut your heart out."

"Make it two."

"I'm serious, because that's what this job does to me. Maybe that's the problem. It's a job, not a mission."

"So what, you gonna call the President, ask him to start a war down here?"

Maro said, "We don't have to ask. When the time is right, we just start killing Americans."

That was three months ago, Maro amazed he'd made it through that many days. Some were okay, interesting, but he looked back on most of them with shame. What a waste of his talents and ambition. The Luna Cartel would be upset, sure. They had big plans for this project, a lot of money into it.

But what would they do with him after, ship him to another site to start it all over? Call him back to Juarez to terrorize the citizens?

No thanks.

Maybe the timing wasn't perfect, but he didn't think it was going to get any better.

Now it was dark enough. He was a mile upriver of the job site, the whole area dark over there so Darwin and his Border friends could hide. Maro used another phone to call Arturo.

"Tell everybody to go," he said. He put the phone in a plastic bag, stowed it and nudged his black inner tube into the Rio, leading the six *salvajes*.

●●●

Darwin took first shift as the rover. Cal had the chair and Gabe was lying on top of the red Conex with the other night scope and his AR. He'd found three tiny sandbags in the shipper when he was looking for a ladder and had them spaced along the rim, one at his right, front, and left. Darwin walked around the corners, checking it all out.

Gabe kept his eye on scope. "The word you're looking for is *fortress.*"

"That is a word." Darwin looked at Marty's trailer, listened but didn't hear anything from inside. "Anybody peek out?"

"Nope. I think it's a sleepover."

"Holler if anybody wants to move next door, I'll walk them over."

"Copy that."

Darwin strolled between the trailers, all the windows black. The generator was off. He looked at the tower site, the shipper down there next to the cleared space, the scene looking like an abandoned lunar landing.

After a while he walked between clumps of scrub toward the Rio, taking his time and getting a feel for the night. He stopped about a hundred yards from the trailers and crouched, his knees going off like bubble wrap. It wasn't quite cold enough for his breath to show up, but it was close.

His eyes were adjusted to the dark now and he could pick out details, not just dark blobs on a less dark background. He identified rocks that would give cover and concealment, defilade depressions, routes back to the higher ground. He kept still and let everything come back to life around him, the lizards and bugs and whatever else clicking over the rocks.

Christine was kicking at the back of his head, trying to get in and make him think about it all, what to do. She always asked him about other women when he was deployed or on the job, grilling him about how many groupies were at the bars and what they said to him, the women in the signals and support squadrons who worshiped the Delta boys.

"I don't know," he'd tell her. "I don't pay attention to them."

Which was true, for the most part, and she'd say, "Yeah right."

Now if she asked him, with this Anna thing going on, he didn't know what he'd say.

Anna thing. Christ, go ahead and plan a full invasion based on one scrap of assumed intel.

Didn't stop Christine from kicking.

Not now, he thought. I need to be relaxed and focus.

Yeah, bullshit. You'd rather blow a door and storm a room full of armed men than talk to your wife. Maybe arrange a sit-down with her, a lawyer if she wanted, and flash-bang the room first. Rappel through the window in full kit. Get it started on familiar ground.

He was running through it, seeing the look on her face when Cal came through the earpiece. "Movement at ten o'clock, one click, three on foot."

"Copy," Darwin said. "Weapons?"

"Unknown."

"Keep me posted." Darwin kept still. He was in line with Cal's twelve o'clock, straight from the trailers to the river. Ten o'clock put the three walkers downriver, beyond the tower site and gulley. One kilometer had them on this side of the Rio, on American soil. He switched to Anna's channel and keyed the mic.

"We see them," she said, her voice low. "Five, three at my eleven and two further out, almost our nine o'clock the way the river bends. All headed this way, trying to be sneaky. They get much closer we can switch to thermal."

"Carrying anything?"

"They have packs on, hard to tell what's in their hands the way they're moving."

"You want help?"

"We're good for now. They head your way we'll sweep down behind them." Anna was on the far side of the gulley, the anchor for the rest of the agents strung out to the southeast, away from the trailers.

"Say the word," Darwin said, and switched channels. He gave Cal and Gabe the details.

"You want crosshairs on these folks?" Cal said.

"Negative, keep a wide scan going."

"Hold on," Gabe said. "I got six—no, seven—coming in at two o'clock. Running toward three. One point five clicks out."

Darwin stayed in a crouch and pivoted on the balls of his feet, faced northwest. "They trying both sides of the site? Looking for a way around?"

Gabe said, "Sheep, guys are dropping off, one at a time. They're forming a skirmish line."

"I see it," Cal said. "Okay, they're coming this way. They aren't trying to go past. This is an assault."

"Coming in," Darwin said, and sprinted toward Marty's trailer.

CHAPTER 12

MARO WAS AT the inland end of the skirmish line, almost at the base of the hill that ran all the way to where Marty parked his big Suburban. He hoped Darwin was in his lawn chair again. This time push him back into the gulley and funnel him down toward the river, let him see what's waiting.

Or pull him and the others away so Arturo could get at the agents, the Anna woman if he could. This mission was about quality, not quantity. Maro wasn't sure killing some security guards would get the right response. He knew about the ones in Fallujah and how the Marines had responded, but the Marines weren't here. Not yet, anyway.

Kill Marty and his engineers, that would get things moving. Until everybody found out what they were doing out here, then it might be good riddance to them.

But a female Border agent, boy oh boy.

His *salvajes* were moving forward too fast, too eager to start shooting, but Maro let them go. He moved further to his left, up the hill, and slowed down a bit. Let them open fire and draw all the attention. Who knows, maybe Darwin will come down the hill and walk right next to him like he did the night before.

Maro tugged his *saperka*, made sure it was loose and ready to come out, just in case.

●●●

Darwin was almost to the trailers when Gabe came through the earpiece. "Got a man coming out." Then Gabe shouted off-mic: "Sir, get back inside please."

"I'm just taking a leak. Marty doesn't want us messing up his bathroom."

"Sir."

"I got it," Darwin said over comms. He saw Jim walking down the stairs, one hand on the railing and the other pressed against the trailer wall. He eased one foot to the next step, brought the other foot and took a deep breath before trying the next one.

"Jim, you gotta get back inside man."

"Whozzat?"

Darwin stopped at the bottom of the stairs. The whiskey cloud rolled past him and made his eyes water. "Jim, back inside until we can secure a route, then we're all going to the Suburban."

"But I gotta piss."

"Piss in your hand, get back inside." Darwin thumped on the trailer. "Marty, Dave, get everybody ready to move."

Jim stood up straight, looked around. "Are they here?"

"Yes, we–"

"Fuck that guy." Jim was staring at the trailer's window, where Marty's desk would be. He waved his middle finger at the window, looked down and saw Darwin standing there.

"You wanna hear something?" He leaned forward and Darwin had to catch him, had to reset his feet to keep the big man from taking them both down. His breath was flammable. For a second Darwin thought Jim was going to kiss him on the cheek.

"You know that bunk you saw, the extra one in our trailer?"

"Jim."

"It's not extra. It's Robbie's."

•••

Maro let his *salvajes* get within five hundred meters of the site before he whistled, high and sharp like a bat. They stopped and found something to get behind. They were spread out, twenty five meters or so between each, and some of them talked in normal voices to the man next door, joking and laughing.

These guys, man. Maro pictured the battlefield from above, where everybody was, and Arturo was the only person on it he didn't want to shoot. When they'd planned the mission, they decided it could go one of three ways. Each one was still possible.

One, Darwin and his team and the Border agents could fall back to the trailers and wait for the raiders to come in. The agents would call for backup and Maro would have to kill as many as possible from a distance before the helicopters showed up.

Two, the security boys and agents could come out to engage. The killing would be easier that way, and the *salvajes* knew to look for chances to take people alive so they could kill them in Mexico, make it worse for America.

Three, Darwin and the agents could pull everyone to the trucks and zoom away. That would be the hardest. If they got away without anyone dying, they might never come back and Maro would have to go back to the old plan, watching people move dirt around. And if Marty was gone, maybe even that would get canceled.

Not the worst thing in the world, but the cartel would probably call him back to Juarez to kill police chiefs or take more land from ranchers.

He pictured it.

Please, just cut my balls off and call it good.

He left his *salvajes* in position and worked his way up the hill toward the big truck to make sure somebody died tonight.

●●●

Darwin stood in front of Jim, who was sitting on the trailer steps, hands covering his face. Every few seconds his body would shake with a sob but he wasn't making any sounds.

Darwin keyed his mic. "Check in."

"Nilla," Cal said. "Six tangos at two o'clock, five hundred meters and holding. They're waiting for something."

"Where's number seven?" Darwin said.

"Ghosted. I'm looking."

"Poppa," Gabe said. Darwin could hear him in stereo, strong through the earpiece and just barely from the top of the shipper. His voice was calm. "I lost him too. Border knows the situation. When're we moving?"

"Standby. Find number seven. Everybody switch to Border's channel."

Jim rocked back and forth on the step, whispering: "I don't know, I don't know."

Darwin hit the mic again. "Ricks, Sheepdog. Status check."

Anna came back: "Five guys hunkered in the rocks and bushes, confirmed firearms. Repeat, armed men, about three hundred meters to the southeast of the tower site."

She sounded tense.

Darwin said, "I recommend you all fall back to the rally point and we extract."

"We called for air support. Awaiting confirmation."

"ETA?"

"Thirty minutes, soonest," she said.

"Pack it up. Meet us at the Suburban, you can ride the running boards to your trucks."

Cal broke in: "Sheepdog, Nilla. We got tangos at the Suburban."

•••

Maro was a little surprised no one had seen him loop around to the parking area—he figured Darwin and his team had night vision technology, and certainly the Border agents did, maybe even thermal—but hey, give credit where it's due. His *salvajes* were good at looking dangerous and holding people's attention.

The *salvajes* were itching to play, some of them out of boredom, which he understood, and some because they wanted to impress him. That was funny. He'd watched them pass the whiskey and quick snorts of cocaine around to get ready for this, a mission they should be able to do with nothing to grow their balls.

He stood behind the big truck and peered down the hill toward the lookout spot with its fancy lawn chair. He couldn't see it but somebody had to be there, close enough to hear anything louder than a hand clap.

Maro crouched and frowned at the rear driver's side wheel. He couldn't believe it—he'd never had to disable a vehicle quietly. Before, it had always been put a burst into the radiator or roll a grenade under the gas tank. Boom, that's done.

So, what, slash the tires? They could roll out of here on the rims, for a while at least, until the rough two-track broke something important.

Cut the gas line. Okay, where is that? He dropped onto his belly and looked at the underside, all steel panels and brackets and bolts. The fucking thing was a tank. He pulled his knife and started cutting things, wires, plastic ties, until he found a tube and cut it, smiling, then smelled windshield washer fluid and cursed the world.

He stood and walked toward the front, thinking there might be a latch to pop the hood. On the way past the driver's door he tugged the handle in case it was unlocked and the truck gave a loud chirp, the lights all blinking once.

Maro froze. He stood there for ten seconds, waiting for someone to shoot at him. If the thing had an alarm, he–

The whole truck exploded into life, horn blowing, lights flashing.

Maro ducked, then felt stupid.

Well, if they want to make some noise.

He walked to the front of the truck and put two bursts from his AK into the radiator. Fluid spilled onto the dirt. He shot the front tires too, the horn and lights still going. Then he ran down the two-track, smiling, looking for the Border Patrol trucks.

●●●

"Okay," Darwin said into the mic, and Gabe hit a button on the key fob to stop the Suburban's alarm.

"Somebody's running," Cal said. "Away, sounds like down the two-track. One guy, must be our number seven. Sneaky bastard."

"He's going for the Border vehicles."

"I can stop that," Cal said.

"Negative, I smell ambush. They know where our chair is; displace toward the gulley. But stay on top of the ridge."

"Moving."

Anna came through: "Nuñez and Foster are circling around toward the vehicles. We're sitting tight. Our five hostiles aren't moving."

"Copy that." Darwin released the mic.

Jim leaned against the trailer, pressing his face against the cool siding.

Darwin said, "Jim, this is known in the industry as 'a bit fucked.' We should be flying toward the highway right now."

"I don't like flying."

The trailer door opened and Dave peeked out. He looked between Darwin and Jim a few times, finally said, "We heard gunshots."

"Suburban's probably dead," Darwin said.

"Oh. Then, how do we get off-site? We're ready to go."

"Now you are, huh? It might not be an option any more."

Dave frowned at Jim's back. "Jim, what are you doing?"

"I'm not talking to you."

"Come on inside. Marty's worried about you."

Jim hooted. "Yeah, I bet he is." He shook his head, rubbing his scalp along the trailer.

"Who's Robbie?" Darwin said.

"Jim, get inside." Dave opened the door and took a step down.

Gabe came through the earpiece. "Sheepdog, Poppa. Six tangos incoming, two o'clock moving from cover to cover. I see three, four long guns. Assume all six are carrying same."

Darwin yanked Jim to his feet and shoved him up the stairs into Dave's arms. He pushed them both through the door and stood in the opening. It was darker inside than out. He couldn't identify faces, but the shapes were there.

"Everybody up, you're going in the Conex. Not *one* fucking peep. I don't know what's going on here, but when we're done saving your lives, I *will* kick the shit out of all of you."

●●●

Maro gave his treatment to the two Border trucks. He stuck his head into the backs, looking for extra night optics or a radio, saw spare tires and tow ropes, jugs of water. He was carrying a road flare to the first gas tank when he heard them coming, two of them unless the rest were very quiet.

He dropped the unlit flare and ducked into the brush along the two-track, moving away from the trucks until he was far enough in, then stopped and crouched behind a thick mesquite trunk. He wanted to hear them talk, see if one was Anna.

●●●

Darwin backed out the door of Marty's trailer and watched the shapes stand up and work toward him. When Brad got to the doorway Darwin told him to wait, then walked down the stairs and scanned the landscape. He moved halfway between the trailer and the shipper, didn't see any close threats.

"Poppa, Sheepdog. Ready to move." He could have shouted to Gabe up on the shipper, but yelling meant panic.

"Clear to move," Gabe said. "Tangos at four hundred meters, incoming."

Darwin kept his body facing out, turned his head and waved at Brad. "Come on. Behind me. Don't run."

Brad emerged, then John and Eric. They looked into the shadows with wide eyes and tight mouths and speed-walked to the shipper. They'd been drinking, though not with Jim's determination. The heavy shipper door was unlocked and unlatched and they swung it far enough to squeeze inside.

Dave and Marty stepped out of the trailer, had a brief conversation on the small platform at the top of the stairs, then came toward Darwin.

"Keep moving, gentlemen."

Marty spoke to his back. "Pat, what's happening out here?"

"Not now, get in the shipper. Where's Jim?"

"On the couch," Dave said. "He was having trouble standing. He'll be along."

"Goddam it."

Marty looked up the hill. "Dave said they shot the Suburban. Is that true?"

"Yes, and we don't know where all these guys are, so let's go."

Marty crossed his arms and looked at Dave. "Are we in real trouble here?"

Darwin stepped back until he was next to them, kept his eyes scanning while he grabbed Marty's collar, jerked him off balance and walked him toward the shipper.

"Now, hey," Dave said.

Darwin put the sole of his boot on Dave's hip and shoved him along too.

"Don't bang on the walls, don't yell for help. We'll let you out when it's safe."

He had them outside the shipper door when Gabe said, "Runner."

Darwin turned and saw Jim thumping around the corner of the trailer, headed down the slope toward the tower site.

"Oh, oh no," Dave said.

Darwin cycled through the options. "Go."

Gabe slid down the ladder and tossed the scope to Darwin. Then he was gone, chasing Jim, his M4 tracking everywhere he looked.

Darwin looked between Marty and Dave. "Buncha fucking two year olds."

Dave opened his mouth and Darwin pointed at him. Dave put his hands up and stepped into the shipper.

Marty said, "Pat, I think some things have changed here. I, I need to make some calls."

Darwin pushed him into the shipper and locked the door.

CHAPTER 13

MARO LISTENED TO the two men talk about their trucks in low voices. They sounded very unhappy, acting like the things were pets or family members. Americans and their trucks.

Hey boys, you lucky I don't have any Semtex. There was some greasy dynamite for the cartel project, but let the stupid farmers blow themselves up with that.

In Afghanistan some of the tribal men, all they wanted was a vehicle. For status or just to make life easier. Maro would leave a vehicle outside a village, goat blood and empty casings splashed around, like the Russians abandoned it after an ambush. He'd sit in the hills and wait until the elders loaded the whole village for a victory lap, then blow the blocks of Semtex strapped under the seats. The Russians asked him what he was doing with all the vehicles.

"Killing the enemy," he told them. "What do you use them for?"

Now he waited for Anna to show up at the trucks. Killing just the two men on this side would be good, but not what he wanted. The best would be to kill them here and take Anna across, show the men had failed to protect her. Get the flood of law and cameras to the border then kill her on the hillside, where the farmer's blood made all the flies gather.

Maro was picturing it, all the Americans standing across the river watching, when he heard one of the men at the trucks mention a helicopter. He called it a chopper. Maro eased his phone out and called Arturo, one ear on the Border agents.

"Where are you?"

"I'm set," Arturo said. "Speak up."

"I can't. They have a helicopter coming. Maybe boats."

"You want to cancel?"

"Yes, call time-out. I'll tell Marty we didn't mean it."

"Sorry."

Maro said, "Where is everybody?"

"The boys are closing the pincers. I think the security team has everyone in the shipper."

"Anna?"

"I don't know."

"Is anyone close enough to grab?"

"Wait."

Maro heard whispering through the phone, then nothing. He peered around the mesquite trunk. The Border agents were using flashlights to look for tracks. If they came into the brush, he'd shoot them.

Arturo said through the phone, "Someone's coming. I'll call you back."

●●●

Darwin decided he would name the incident report for this Operation Clusterfuck: Part 2. He made sure Marty and the others weren't going to bang on the shipper walls, then keyed his mic.

"Poppa, Sheepdog. Status."

"Jim's heading for the blue Conex," Gabe said. "Calling

for somebody named Robbie. Drunks, man. I forgot how fast they are."

"Thought you left 'em all in Detroit?"

"He's at the box, looking for the door. Thinks he's supposed to hide in this one."

The gunshots cracked up the slope and Darwin had the ridiculous thought that Gabe was firing warning shots over Jim's head, but these were loud, unsupressed, then Gabe yelled through the earpiece: "Contact, contact at the box."

Cal said, "Who's shooting?"

"Not me." Gabe's breathing sped up. "Jim! Jim, it's Gabe, I'm coming in. Don't shoot."

Darwin scoped down the hill but couldn't see a damn thing, too much scrub in the way. He panned right but couldn't find the tangos to the north either.

Gabe said, "Jim's hit, he's shot."

"Get–" Darwin got cutoff by the gunshots, three of them, from the blue shipper.

"Poppa, status."

Nothing. Darwin stuffed the scope in his chest pouch and got the M4 up, ran two steps before he remembered Marty and the others.

"*Fuck.* Nilla, where are you?"

"Top of the gulley."

"I need you at the blue shipper. Shooters there."

"On my way."

●●●

Maro heard the shots, then the two men at the trucks running toward the trailers. Whatever Arturo was doing, it was good. Maro waited until the footsteps faded, then he slipped out to the trucks and across the road. The agents had come from that way, maybe the arroyo or beyond it.

Now they were running down the hill and he headed to where Anna was, by herself or with her partner, which would be no problem.

● ● ●

Darwin was halfway up the ladder when his earpiece clicked.

"Nuñez and Foster coming in, we're coming down the hill to the trailers, don't fire."

"Copy," Darwin said and slid to the ground. "Rally at the Conex."

When he saw the two shapes come around the corner of Marty's trailer he said, "Can you guys stay here, cover the civilians? They're in the box."

"Who's shooting?" Nuñez said. He was out of breath.

"My guy's down there, I gotta find out. You good?"

"We're good, go."

Darwin ran toward the tower site, knowing this part would look bad in the incident report. The whole thing was bad, but Hank would freak about him leaving the principle. Technically Jim was a client too, but Hank's first concern would be for the guy signing the checks.

"Nilla, Sheepdog. On my way to you."

"Copy. Ricks, I'm coming out of the gulley. Please don't shoot me."

Anna said, "I see you. I can't see shit at the tower site. The five guys are still coming in, slower now, about two hundred fifty meters out. They stopped and had a chat after the shots."

"Where they headed?" Darwin said. He was halfway to the blue Conex, jumping over rocks and cutting around cactus.

"Angling for the stretch between you and the river. They

might loop around, try to cut you off."

"Let us know. Poppa, status."

Still nothing.

"Jim, can you hear me?"

Dead air.

Darwin hit the semi-cleared swath around the tower site, loose gravel crunching under his boots. He stepped toward the back corner of the Conex and saw Cal wave from the far side. Darwin got to the corner and pointed toward the front. Cal disappeared around his corner and they swept down the sides. There was no sound around them or inside the box.

"Going bright," Cal said through the earpiece.

Darwin put his hand over the Streamlight lens, mounted at a forty-five degree angle down off the top rail, and hit the switch with his trigger thumb. The skin over the lens glowed pink. He cut around the front corner and saw the far door was ajar, three feet of blackness waiting for him. Cal leaned out from the other side of the door, keeping himself blocked from whoever was inside, and nodded.

Half my paycheck for a flash-bang, Darwin thought.

He took his hand off the lens and sliced through the door, yelling, "*Down down down,*" his voice bouncing off the ribbed metal.

He hugged the far wall, his beam sweeping along the steel toward the back. Cal was at his shoulder then cut left into the corner made by the closed door. Between them they had the entire space covered.

It was empty.

CHAPTER 14

MARTY THOUGHT HIS trailer had been dark. Now he put his hand an inch from his face and could only see shapes floating across the black screen, something he'd have to ask his optometrist about next time he was home.

He pulled the cheap cell phone out and hit a button to light the screen. Dave was next to him. Brad and Eric and John were further into the box, looking like they were starting down a long dark hallway.

"I'm gonna throw up," Brad said.

Marty said, "Just sit down. Everybody, find a seat."

"Where's Jim?"

"They're getting him, it's fine."

"Those were gunshots out there."

"It's hard to tell, these acoustics." Marty had a quick scene of the three engineers rushing him, the stress too much. Dave would stand there, ask if something was wrong while they rolled him up.

Nah. They wouldn't make a move without Jim to poke them. Maybe it was good he wasn't in the box. Marty checked the phone for a signal, got no bars inside the steel walls.

Dave shuffled close. "What did Maro say when he called?"

"I don't know. He said there's a new plan. I don't know

what the hell he's doing."

"Maybe it's somebody else. Making a move on the project, or against Luna."

"No, it's him."

Eric stacked boxes and tool cases to make three seats. The engineers sat down, leaving Marty and Dave to fend for themselves.

Eric said, "Was Jim going to the blue Conex?"

"Stop," Marty said. "I don't want to think about it."

Dave put his hands in his pockets, rocked onto his heels. "If the agents go in there, or Darwin's team, we'll need a story."

●●●

Darwin and Cal walked the inside walls toward the back of the Conex, boots thumping on the steel. Their beams found a black mat, four feet square, in the middle of the floor a few feet away from the back wall.

They got closer and Darwin said, "That's a hole."

He moved along the wall until he was next to the hole, then crouched, Cal across from him. Their beams pushed all the shadows out of the hole, which was cut in the floor of the Conex. The shaft walls were reinforced with boards. Dust boiled up through the opening. Darwin could hear people moving fast down there, getting quieter.

"The fuck is this?" Cal said.

"Poppa, you down there?"

In the hole, a man coughed.

"Who is that?" Darwin said.

"Help. Help me."

It was weak.

Cal mouthed: Poppa?

Darwin shrugged. Could be Gabe, Jim, or somebody waiting at the bottom of the shaft with that AK pointed up, waiting for a fat white face to poke over the side.

Cal raised his eyebrows and Darwin nodded.

They leaned over the opening and filled the shaft with light, ten feet straight down where they could see an aluminum extension ladder lying on the dark dirt floor.

"Poppa, Sheepdog. That you?"

"Guys . . ."

"Jim?"

"I'm bleeding here."

He was somewhere close.

"Is anybody with you?"

"They left me."

Darwin said, "Jim, where is our man? Where is Gabe?"

"He's gone. They took him." They heard a sob, then a gasp. "Guys, I'm hurt bad."

Darwin let his M4 hang from its sling. He put his feet in the hole. Cal leaned in from his side and held his hands out, crossed at the wrist. Darwin crossed his and grabbed Cal's. Cal pulled him forward then eased him down so Darwin could brace his boots and back against opposite walls of the shaft.

Darwin's knees protested and he gritted his teeth at them. When he was locked in, Cal knelt at the edge and pointed his M4 through the space between Darwin's shins.

"Tell Anna we got a situation down here."

He stepped down one boot at a time, braced, slid his back down the wall.

Again.

●●●

Darwin's heels were pressed against the last board. It was a great time for anybody who didn't like him to shoot his ass off.

"Drop and clear," Cal said from above. In his beam the floor looked to be about six feet down from the bottom of the shaft.

Darwin said, "How we doing Jim?"

"Shit."

Darwin dropped to the floor and had the M4 up, stepping out of Cal's line of fire and sweeping the Streamlight in a full circle. The tunnel was six feet high and six wide. He had to duck to keep his helmet from scraping the roof, reinforced with some kind of synthetic decking material. The walls were faced with the same, ten-inch slats of it stacked on edge floor to ceiling and secured by vertical posts every eight feet.

Darwin got his bearings. Toward the Rio, the tunnel stretched beyond his flashlight beam. The space in that direction felt deep, cold, endless. Behind him, up the hill into Texas, the excavation went twenty feet and stopped. Supports were in place halfway up the dirt walls. Shovels and picks and a sledge hammer leaned against a wheel barrow, the tire caked with mud.

Jim sat against the wall, one hand draped over a wheelbarrow handle. He squinted in the white LED beam. His other forearm and hand were pressed to his stomach.

"Hey, come on. Who's that?"

"Jim, what's happening here?"

"Can you take a look at this?" He took the hand away from his stomach and showed Darwin a dark red stain like a cummerbund.

"Hold on man." Darwin pulled the aluminum ladder up and threaded it into the shaft, kicked it into place.

"Coming down," Cal said. He slid down the sides of the ladder, got his weapon up and scanned the area. "Ah, come on."

"I know," Darwin said.

Cal pulled the med kit out and knelt next to Jim, eased him flat on the ground.

Darwin kept his eyes and beam down the tunnel. Faint sounds drifted to him, unidentifiable. "Okay bud, I need details."

"Am I going to die?"

"How dare you," Cal said. To Darwin: "Bullet wound, right abdomen, through-and-through. Stable, but we gotta ship him."

Darwin stepped back and knelt by Jim's head. "Where is Gabe?"

"They took him that way."

"Who, the cartel?"

Jim nodded. He was sober now.

"Is he hurt?"

"I don't know. He didn't sound good. I think they shot him too."

"But he is alive," Darwin said.

"Man, I really don't know. I'm sorry. *Fuck*, what are you doing?"

"Hold still," Cal said.

Darwin asked Jim, "Does this tunnel go into Mexico?"

"Yes."

"And you knew about it. Marty, everybody."

He laughed, grimaced. "We designed it for them, made sure it was safe. Wouldn't cave in."

"Okay, why?"

"Cash money, man. And they have Robbie, case we changed our minds. Which we did, but, you know. Too late now."

"Robbie is an engineer."

"Yeah, he's my friend."

"Where do they have him?"

"Fuck if I know," Jim said. "I don't even know if he's alive."

"When did they take him?"

"No, they didn't *take* him. Marty *gave* him to them. It was his fucking idea."

Cal raised his eyebrows at Darwin.

"You gotta get him back," Jim said. To Cal: "Can you give me some morphine? Just knock me out. I don't wanna be awake for any of this. Wake me up when Robbie is home and safe."

Cal pulled a styrette from his thigh pouch.

Darwin put a hand up. "Jim, where does this tunnel come out?"

"The blue Conex."

"The other end."

"Far side of the hill, a little bit west."

Darwin nodded. Cal stuck Jim with the styrette and his body relaxed, melted toward the floor.

"Am I still awake?" he said.

Cal moved next to Darwin. "Well?"

"You got your passport?"

CHAPTER 15

DARWIN KEPT HIS beam down the tunnel while Cal lifted Jim across his shoulders and got him up the ladder, the aluminum bowing under the weight. Darwin followed them up and scanned the tower site and desert beyond while they moved toward the trailers, Cal not even breathing hard from the work.

Darwin hit his mic. "Ricks, Sheepdog, we have a situation. Meet at the trailers. Leave your team in place."

"Who's shooting?"

"Not on the air," he said, telling her the radios weren't secure. They were, but he didn't want to tell everyone what they were doing, case the Border guys tried to stop them. When they got close to the trailers Darwin yelled for Nuñez and Foster, "Friendlies coming in, don't shoot."

"The fuck's going on?" one of them said in the darkness, maybe fifty yards away.

"Standby. And don't let anybody out of that shipper."

Cal eased Jim onto the steps of their trailer and checked the wound. Darwin kept going up the stairs, got into the trailer and started loading up on ammunition. He threaded the suppressor onto his .45, secured it in the holster, then pulled the long Pelican crate out for Cal, set it on the table and stepped out of the trailer to see Anna coming around the corner.

She sped up when she saw Jim sprawled out and bloody, pulled a glove off and pressed fingers against his neck, looked up at Darwin. "What's happening?"

Darwin asked Cal, "How is he?"

"Loopy, stable."

"We got him."

Cal stepped into the trailer to gear up. Anna reached for her radio.

"Stop," Darwin said. "This man's been shot and needs medical attention, but him and all the rest—Marty, all of them—are now in your custody. They're digging a goddam tunnel from Mexico for the cartel and Gabe just got snatched into it. We're getting him back."

"Wait, what?"

"Fall back on this area and wait for your backup. We run into any shooters out there, we'll handle them."

"You can't go into Mexico."

"You got your five hostiles coming in from the southeast, six in a skirmish line out here to the northwest and one loner behind you shooting everything up. Bet that's our Lobo. Guy knows my name because goddam Marty gave it to him."

"Hey. Listen to me."

"You remember me saying I can be an asshole?"

Cal stepped out of the trailer with his M4 slung across his back and the SR-25 sniper rifle in his hands, the rifle mean-looking with the long suppressor and Leupold 10X scope with AN/PVS-22 night vision system he'd paid for himself.

Anna put her palms toward both of them. "No, you guys."

"Anna," Darwin said. "We're going." He clicked his mic. "All Border agents, this is Sheepdog. Two friendlies heading for the river, do not engage." He let go of the mic, looked at Jim. "Jim, what does Robbie look like?"

"Robbie."

"Do you have a photograph?"

"Trailer."

Cal was already moving.

Anna watched him go, brought her radio up to her mouth. Darwin waited to see if she'd tell her team, Go ahead and shoot these guys, but she didn't hit the button.

He said, "Did you know anything about this?"

"Fuck you. I still don't know what *this* is. A tunnel? You and Cal need to calm down, wait for our support to get here."

"No time."

Something crashed inside the engineers' trailer, Cal in there tossing things out of his way.

Anna said, "I understand your concern for Gabe."

"Concern." It wasn't the right word for it, but he liked it better than *panic*.

"I really do. But I can*not* allow you to violate the border."

"Anna, it's a line on a map. They don't care about it, why should I?"

Cal came back with a photograph. The two of them flipped their night optics down, looked at the faces and found the new one: square head, blond crewcut, slanted smile.

Anna pulled her Maglite.

"No lights," Cal said. To Darwin: "We got what we need?"

"Hold on." No time to waste, but this last thing could make a difference.

"Tick tock."

"I know."

Darwin moved to the red Conex. Cal was next to him, Anna trailing behind with the radio still in her hand. Darwin opened the door and stepped inside. Said to Cal, "Close it behind me. Nobody in."

●●●

Darwin looked at Marty and Dave through the night optics, both of them staring in his direction but not fixing on anything, scanning what had to be pitch black to them.

Marty put a hand out. "Who's that?"

"They have Gabe."

"Hey, Pat. Do you have a flashlight?"

"Who are we fighting out there?"

"Ah, it'd really help if I could see you."

Darwin hit him in the belly, a short hook that dropped him to a knee and had him making uncontrolled sounds. He sagged against Dave's legs. Dave reached down, patted Marty's head until he found his shoulders and tried to help him up. Marty dropped lower.

"What did you do?" Dave said.

Darwin shoved him against the wall. "I'm asking you too Dave. Feel free to speak up."

Dave's eyes were huge, his hands up to cover his face.

"Anybody in here," Darwin said. "Who are we fighting?"

A voice came from the back of the Conex, behind a stack of tool cases. "His name's Maro."

"You shut the fuck up!" Marty said from the floor. "Pat, you're fired. Pack your shit and get out of here. Get off my job site, you're tresspassing. Anna!"

"This isn't your job site anymore. It's my battlefield. It's down to friend or foe. Pick one."

Marty pushed up to one knee. "I don't know what you're talking about."

Darwin spoke to the engineers behind the boxes. "I don't have time to come looking for you. Jim's been shot and we're going over to bring Robbie home. Start talking."

Marty said, "Anybody talks to Pat is fired."

"You're begging to get shot."

"It's the cartel," a voice said.

"Who's that, Brad?" Marty stood up, his arms crossed over his stomach. "You just fucked yourself, buddy."

Brad said, "The guy in charge is Maro, that's the only name we know besides the workers, but that's all they are. They don't want to be here. Is Jim hurt bad?"

"Yes."

"Is he going to die?"

"What can you tell me about Robbie? Do you know where he is?"

"No. You can bring him home?"

"Who's Robbie?" Marty said. "We don't know anybody with that name."

It took everything Darwin had not to put a round through him, at least choke him for a while. "Anything I need to know about the tunnel? Any booby traps, dead ends, choke points?"

Voices mumbled. Then: "I don't think so. It's a straight shot all the way through."

"This Maro, he carries a little shovel, an entrenching tool?"

"That's him."

Marty said, "Goddamit, shut your mouth back there." He stumbled in that direction, found some boxes and pushed them over. Almost fell, then turned toward Darwin with his hands out to protect himself. "Pat, we don't know anything about anybody out there. That's my statement. Now you're banned from the premises. Get Anna in here."

"If Gabe dies," Darwin had to talk through his teeth to keep from yelling. "I get back, you and I are going to have a very short meeting."

"What's that supposed to mean?"

Marty and Dave both jumped when Darwin thumped the door. He stepped out and latched it behind him, turned and got moving downhill. Cal fell in next to him.

Anna ran in front and tried to slow them down. "What happened in there? Did you assault anyone?"

"I know you have to ask that, but you know I'm gonna lie, so what's the point?"

"Darwin, stop. You go across, I have to arrest you."

"That's fine. Just do it when we get back."

They moved past her and picked up speed. Darwin ignored his knees as he and Cal sprinted toward the blue Conex and the tunnel.

•••

Maro crouched near the lawn chair and some empty food containers, watched two dark shapes run away toward the tower site—hopefully not his Anna—wondered if they were chasing Arturo back into the tunnel. Go in there, man, you stupid. Some of the *salvajes* liked to stay down there, keep an eye on the diggers and fuck the women when the urge hit. Called themselves *cavernícola*, caveman, and they were right.

When the two shapes were gone he moved closer to the arroyo, listening hard for voices and movement and almost swore out loud when his phone vibrated. He backtracked to a large rock and squatted next to it. He'd turned the screen light off but knew who it would be.

"What?"

"Where are you?" Arturo said.

"Top of the arroyo. Two people are coming to you from the trailers."

"No, I'm out, across the river. We have one of them."

Maro's eyebrows went up. "Which one?"

"One of the security men, the darker one."

Shit. "Is he alive?"

"Yes, we shot him but not too bad. The boys are thumping on him."

"Tell them to stop. And don't kill him until I get there."

"You're coming across?"

"Soon. Watch out for the two headed your way. It will be

Darwin and the beard, coming for their man."

"The cavemen are still in the tunnel."

"Thumping their chests and snorting their balls. I think they in for a surprise—these two aren't farmers."

He put the phone away and listened, all the night creatures quiet while the real beasts fought it out. A man yelled something from down by Marty's trailer and a woman answered. Well, this is all right. Maro pulled the phone back out and called Arturo, gave him the orders. Then he kept his head below the top of the scrub and started working his way down toward Anna's voice.

●●●

Darwin and Cal cleared the blue Conex again, the ladder still sticking up out of the tunnel entrance. They were using night optics now, no flashlights. The infrared illuminator on Darwin's M4 gave them plenty of light, everything washed in shades of green. He tested the thumb pad and the aiming laser cut a beam through the dust.

Cal said, "We both go down, pretty easy to clamp us from both ends."

"You going swimming?"

"I find the other end in time, we'll have whoever's down there trapped."

"I might be out of radio contact down there. You find Gabe, get him back over here. I'll find you."

"ROE?"

Shit, Darwin thought, this Maro guy had made it clear: rules of engagement were nil. "You kill whoever you have to."

"See you soon." Cal moved to the Conex door, checked the area outside, and was gone.

Darwin sat on the edge of the hole, grabbed the ladder

and kept the M4 pointed into the tunnel as he went down, again waiting for the explosion of gunfire when his feet passed into the space. It didn't come, just his breathing and fast steps as he moved away from the ladder and into the tunnel toward the Rio.

It smelled damp and there was a hum coming from somewhere. The floor was sheets of plywood with curbs of mud and dirt on each side. The tunnel angled down, followed the slope of the land toward the river, and gave a small window of what was ahead. Anybody was in front of him he'd see their feet first. Darwin turned the IR illuminator off. The night optics still worked, but there was zero ambient light and no light sources ahead. Pitch black.

He turned the IR on and could see everything, his private flashlight, and moved forward with a mental image of Gabe's face, head, silhouette. Anybody showed up who didn't fit that was going to die in the dark.

●●●

Maro was close to the back of Marty's trailer, listening. People were walking around the other end, back and forth to the red Conex at his two o'clock, whispering to each other and talking into radios. He could hear Anna and tried to match her voice to her footsteps, figure out where she was.

He loved that Americans were so predictable. Once you could predict your enemy you could see into the future, like magic. Some of the tribes he'd fought, it took a while to see how they worked and where the buttons were. Take a woman from one tribe, they shrug and go back to moving rocks around. Take a goat? Shit, run for your life.

But Americans, they put it right out there for you. Don't mess with our women. Don't mess with our troops. Or cars.

Giving instructions on how to start a war with them.

He moved closer to the trailer and got ready for what would happen next, two ways it could go. One was perfect, the other a pain in the ass but still no problem. He was listening to Anna talk on her radio, hoping she'd get the ETA on her helicopter when the gunfire started, Arturo doing a good job passing the orders along to the *salvajes* out past the red Conex.

They fired in bursts like he'd shown them, not the full-mag spray that had them shooting into outer space. Maro moved to the back corner of the Conex to put the steel box between him and the bullets. A few slugs thumped into the far side and Maro heard men yelling inside, heavy things falling and scraping on the floor.

Anna and the two men with her scrambled around and fired back in a pretty disciplined manner, calling out muzzle flashes and telling everyone when they were moving. Maro rested his back against the shipper and wished they'd pour it on a little more so when his men fell back it would seem right, but then he heard one of the male agents yell that they're running, the chickenshits are running, and Maro shook his head. Of course, why wouldn't they run from the scary uniforms and haircuts?

Then he heard Anna say, "You guys push the perimeter out, make sure they aren't flanking us. Stay together."

A man said, "You're good here?"

"Fine, go."

Maro heard two people move away into the scrub, then it was just him and Anna.

●●●

Darwin could see dark smears on the plywood floor, impossible to tell if it was blood or just water with the night optics, but the way it spattered and had drag marks through it, he figured he was looking at Gabe's blood. Not enough to make him think Gabe was bleeding out, but any blood outside the body wasn't great.

He moved forward, kept the M4 and IR light sweeping. The ground under the plywood started to squish and the wall panels showed dark stains from moisture. He saw hoses lying in the mud along the bottom of the walls, stopped and heard a soft hissing under the hum that was getting louder. Somewhere ahead they had a pump siphoning groundwater out. Good, cover any noise he made.

He stepped ahead twenty more feet and saw that the walls and floor of the tunnel transitioned into a ribbed pipe about six feet in diameter. This would be the section that went under the Rio, the hum turning into a growl. Two men stood at Darwin's end of the pipe, thick guys holding AR-15s—yes, and one of them was Gabe's. In the fraction of a second Darwin scanned them, he saw one guy had a lighter up, ready to flick, the other one holding a hand on him to wait while he tried to listen, head cocked.

Darwin shot them both, the suppressor coughing, two in the chest of the listener and a headshot for the lighter, then one in his chest as he fell. They dropped straight to the ground and landed in a tangle. Darwin crouched next to them and patted, found cell phones but no radios or Russian entrenching tools, hoping to get lucky. Damn.

The plywood sheets were ripped to narrower strips for the floor of the pipe, not as level and tilting here and there when he put his weight down. Darwin kept the IR and his eyes as far ahead as possible—two guys at this end, probably more at the other. The spiraled ribs of the pipe played a little funhouse havoc with his vision until he thought of it as a rifle barrel, making him the bullet.

That's about right.

●●●

Marty sat on something cold and hard in the pitch black of the Conex box and listened to the engineers restacking their tool crate bunker. Focus on that noise, not the gunfire outside, and figure out what the hell to do about Darwin and Agent Anna when this was over.

Fingers touched his shoulder, neck. "Marty?"

"Yeah, Dave."

Dave stepped close, his breathing still fast from Darwin's attack. "You okay?"

"What do you think? My ribs might be shattered."

"You think Jim's really been shot?"

"Christ Dave, I don't know. Don't just bring me problems, huh? You have any solutions?"

"Not yet."

"You want to hear mine?"

"Do I?" Dave said.

"I doubt it." Marty pulled him closer. "We pray Maro and his animals kill Darwin, Anna, all of them. Even Jim, any loose ends."

"Any?"

They both listened to the engineers dragging and piling equipment in the dark.

"All," Marty said. "We blow our end of the tunnel and get the hell out of here, leave Maro to fight the US military by himself, because that's who's coming if he gets his way."

"Jesus."

"There are a few Saudis owe me a favor. We can go there."

"What about the company?"

"As—you know what, you're a goddam good assistant,

Dave—as long as that tunnel gets buried and the loose ends get handled, we should be good. Who's going to tattle? Maro? The cartel?"

"They might, their infrastructure starts getting wiped out by drone attacks and night raids."

"Not these guys." Marty used his tone: this is fact. Maybe Dave was right, but they couldn't form a plan around mights and maybes. "Listen. If Maro loses out there, we have to be prepared to handle things."

"Handle?"

"Maro and his guys get killed, their weapons will be lying around."

"Come on. Marty."

"Dave, we'll be seen as traitors. In fucking *Texas*. No prison. Death penalty. I think they still hang people here."

Dave was quiet. Marty pictured him pursing his lips like he did when there weren't any good options.

Marty said, "How many can you take down?"

"I've never fired a gun in my life."

"They won't see it coming."

"Still, never pulled a trigger Marty."

"Watch your tone, bud. Tell you what. If there's less than ten left alive, I'll do it myself. Not counting the ones in here. More than that, I'm gonna need your help."

"This has gone completely sideways."

"Dave, can I count on you?"

After a while, Dave said, "Yes."

CHAPTER 16

DARWIN CAME TO the other end of the pipe, the walls framed with boards and posts like they were back where he started.

Back in the U.S., he thought, which made this Mexico.

Well, let's make this fast, nobody has to know.

The tunnel sloped up, steeper than the drop down had been, cutting into the hill he'd been looking at since last night. Christ, had it only been a day? Darwin wasn't a fan of fighting uphill, couldn't think of anybody who was, but the view ahead was clear.

The hum got quieter as he went up but was being replaced by something else, mechanical sounds bouncing off the walls toward him. He passed sections of the tunnel that had been carved through rock, no boards on the walls or roof. Made him wonder how long they'd been working on this, and move a little faster, thinking it could all come down on top of him.

Going into caves in Afghanistan, he'd figured they'd been there for centuries and were safe enough, except when they'd gone in after the JDAM bunker busters. Then it was watch your step and nobody sneeze.

The floor and walls got drier as he climbed and he could see the fresh blood trail again, one big dark splotch with a bootprint right in the middle. Not Gabe's boot. Up ahead the tunnel angled down, made a horizon Darwin couldn't see beyond, just the tunnel roof showing in his IR beam. He crouched as he approached the angle, kept his head below the horizon until he was kneeling then took a peek.

Four of them twenty yards away, shit, just sitting on crates with a little fluorescent lantern to make them blind beyond ten yards. They were chatting and rubbing their rifles. The closest one had a Bowie knife, kept stabbing it into the wooden crate he was on. Darwin checked the area, no sign of Gabe alive or dead but the dark stains led all the way to the four clowns.

Gabe was somewhere on the other side of them. Hopefully this Robbie too.

Darwin tried his mic, tapped it once to see if Cal would tap back.

Nothing.

Darwin stepped over the horizon and moved in fast, kept his night optics away from the lantern so he wouldn't go blind. When he was five feet from the edge of the lantern's light he put a round into it, blew it apart with a flash then kept moving and cycled through the targets:

A burst into Bowie's face.

Up a degree, three into the man behind Bowie, dust puffing off his chest.

Other side of the tunnel, a man with huge eyes and his mouth open, nobody Darwin knew. A burst into the head.

Beyond him a man just starting to crouch, wincing and looking past Darwin who was two feet away and felt the air punch out of the guy's lungs when the rounds hit him center mass. Darwin put one into his head and crouched behind a crate in case someone further along decided to open up.

Nothing. The bodies around him were silent. He went to each one, found phones and coke and some church beads. Gabe's body armor and company cell phone were stuffed between a crate and the tunnel wall, the vest soaked with blood and showing where rounds had dug grooves vertically along the Kevlar.

Darwin pictured it, Gabe looking down into the tunnel from the blue Conex and getting a shock of automatic fire. The blood on the vest told Darwin Gabe had been hit in the neck or head. Darwin patted the vest and got ready to move, then saw what was stenciled on the side of the crate:

Peligro!

Dinimita

There were also jagged black explosions and skulls with crossbones stenciled on the wood for folks who couldn't read Spanish, or at all. Darwin looked in the other crates, found blasting caps and some detonating cord, couldn't believe the idiots heaped on the floor had been sitting on them.

Then he really saw what was in front of him, the opportunity, and hoped he had time.

●●●

Cal was in Mexico.

The dirt, scrub, rocks, all of it were exactly the same as the other side of the Rio, but there was a different feeling now, a tactical awareness he hadn't switched on until he'd come out of the water about a quarter mile downstream from where he'd gone in.

He was near the top of the hill, crouched and leaning into a group of rocks stuck into the hillside, listening. The river slid along below and made some white noise, the only thing he heard until gunfire popped across the border up near the trailers.

Shit. He thought about Anna and the two Border agents, flipped the lever on the night vision system and tried to get a look through the scope. The trailers were about eight hundred yards away, shapes moving but no way to identify friendlies. The gunfire rolled to him with a slight delay—even if the hostiles were using AKs, impossible to tell which shape the sound came from.

More gunfire cracked much closer to him, about three hundred yards. He panned right and found the five hostiles who'd come from downstream toward Anna'a original skirmish line. They were ducking behind rocks and mesquite trunks, popping out to loose a volley at the Border agents strung out along the top of the hill near the gulley. If they hit a damn thing it'd be pure luck, but a lucky bullet didn't feel any different than an aimed one.

Cal watched for a few seconds and recognized the maneuver, something the insurgents in Iraq and the AQ and Taliban did all the time in the Afghan mountains. Fire and fall back, fire and fall back, but not to disengage. These cartel guys were trying to pull the Border agents away into something they'd set up.

Dammit. He'd already abandoned the principle and the Border agents at the trailers, least he could do was help these guys out.

Hold on Gabe, be there in a few.

He hit his throat mic, whispered, "Nilla here. Who's in charge on the southeast ridge?"

"Molina. What's happening at the trailers?"

"Unknown, send some guys that way. Confirm all your people are at the top of the ridge."

"Roger that, we're all up here."

"Don't come down the hill. Nilla out."

Cal lined up the guy on the left, closest to the tower site, and squeezed. The bullet hit him between the shoulder blades, knocked him flat and made the guy next to him look over, turn that way. Cal shot him under his left arm, through-and-through the chest cavity, dead before he landed.

The other three hadn't noticed, kept hopping and popping at Molina and the Border agents, who were shooting back but not hitting anyone. Cal took a moment to listen to his surroundings, case anyone had heard his chatter or suppressed shots and was coming in on him. In the Teams he'd always had a spotter, didn't have to worry about it.

Nothing.

He went back to the scope, found the third guy who still hadn't noticed his two buddies weren't shooting anymore, too busy holding his rifle over the top of a rock and firing a burst. Cal aimed his shot for the guy's center mass, watched him duck as the round came in to knock most of his head off.

That'll work too.

The last two must have realized something new was happening, maybe heard the skull impact. They started running to Cal's right, away from the tower site, this a real retreat and not the baiting they'd been doing.

Cal hit his mic. "Molina, Nilla. Do not pursue those runners. Fall back on the trailers and help Anna."

"Copy that. What's your twenty?"

I'm in fucking Mexico. "Nilla out."

He led the slowest runner too much, put a round just in front of him. Adjusted and watched the next one go in his right shoulder blade, send him tumbling face-first into the dirt.

The last one ran faster, zigzagged through the scrub and cactus and ended up running straight toward Cal, who put the crosshairs on his face and watched the bullet drop to hit him between the collarbones. He fell and didn't move again.

Cal collected his brass, six empty casings, stuffed them in an elastic pouch so they wouldn't clink around, then listened. When he didn't hear any movement near him he eased out of the rocks and headed for the ridge. Somewhere on the other side was a tunnel, and Gabe was probably getting pissed having to wait this long to get rescued.

Cal kept that image in his head as he moved, Gabe tapping his foot and checking his watch, because to think about Gabe along with what he'd seen insurgents do to prisoners and what these cartels had been doing to everyone —that was too much.

●●●

Maro heard the gunfire out past the arroyo, then the return fire of the Border agents and thought, Here we go.

He stepped around the corner of the shipper and moved toward the front, could see Anna's silhouette standing there in front of the shipper door looking left, right, left, right, her troops surrounded but pushing the enemy away.

Sure they are.

He was ten feet from her when the shooting near the arroyo started to get quieter. Maro stopped. He knew the sound of his shooters and heard it go from five to three, the Border agents still shooting back but that was another sound to him, one he filtered out.

Then it went from three to two, then none.

Were they running already?

The Border agent guns went silent too. If his *salvajes* had killed them all that was fine, but not part of the plan, and Jesus, he'd never hear the end of it from them, how they'd defeated America.

Maro heard Anna's radio click and a man's voice say, "Ricks, Molina. We're coming to you, leaving two here on the ridge."

"Copy that. Stay north of the trailers, we got shooters to the southwest."

"ETA on the chopper?"

"Still waiting for confirmation. Assholes."

Maro was three feet away from her, the *saperka* in his left hand and his back pressed against the side of the shipper. He waited for them to sign off. Let this Molina know Anna was in trouble, he'd come even faster.

"Ricks out," Anna said, and Maro eased the *saperka* up to shoulder-height, got ready to turn the corner and bring the tool around in an arc when Anna stepped to her right, away from him and started to open the shipper door.

●●●

Marty stood up when he heard the door hardware squealing and clanking, told Dave, "Get ready."

Get ready yourself. He shook his hands out and picked up the short piece of rebar he'd kicked when he was trying to find a place to sit and wait. The right door opened wide enough for someone to step in and put the thick door between them and the shooting that seemed to be getting farther away. The silhouette was a short person wearing a knit cap, carrying an automatic rifle but not pointing it anywhere.

"You guys okay in here?"

Anna. Marty heard Dave give a little groan, the old guy not used to attacking women.

Marty said, "Sure, long as you don't let Darwin back in here."

"We can talk about that later."

"You're damn right." Keep her thinking there will be a later. "What's the situation?"

"I'm still not clear on that, but Jim's been shot and I think you have some explaining to do."

"I do?"

"Marty, that's enough. You all consider yourselves under arrest until I have time to sort this out. Now do you know who we're dealing with out here?"

"You don't know who you're shooting at?" Her rifle was just hanging by some kind of sling across her chest—she didn't even have her hand on the grip where the trigger was. Marty pressed the rebar against his leg. "Let me take a look."

He stepped toward the door.

Anna stayed in the opening, put a hand up. "No, stay in here. Marty, move back."

"You want my help or not?"

He was almost close enough, thinking that if this dumb girl didn't understand what she was forcing him into, didn't get what he had on the line here, that was her problem. The sharp end of the rebar would go into her neck easy enough, then once she was down he could use her gun on her.

"Marty, step back."

"What's the matter?"

He squeezed the rebar, stepped and had it ready to go, just waiting for his foot to land when a shape moved in behind Anna and a blur came down on her head—*pang*—and she dropped to her knees. She grabbed the edge of the closed door, tried to turn and the shape punched her in the face, a solid thud that sent her all the way to the ground.

CHAPTER 17

DARWIN PLAYED THE det cord out behind him through the tunnel and saw the fresh blood trail getting smaller, Gabe either bleeding out or clotting. If he was dead, Darwin couldn't think why these guys would keep dragging him, unless they wanted to make a show out of the dead American, put his head on a spike.

Darwin imagined going to see Gabe's wife and daughters if that happened, them looking at the man whose job it had been to keep Gabe the husband and father safe. He shook that off when he came to another transition in the tunnel, the walls and roof opening up into a large space, a cave, and on the far side an opening about as big as a two-car garage. Past that he could see starlight and landscape.

The inside of the cave was big enough to hold a new but dusty pickup truck on one side and pallets of the tunnel's decking material and posts on the other. Tools and wheelbarrows leaned against the wall, everything crusty with mud. He leaned an empty pallet against the tunnel entrance and braced it with a few boards. Wouldn't stop much, but would let him know if anybody opened his back door.

He looped the det cord behind the full pallets and carried it close to the cave mouth, crouched there and listened while he finished up, concealed his work under a few empty burlap sacks.

He tapped his throat mic.

Cal came back, a whisper: "Nilla."

Darwin kept as quiet as he could. "You find him?"

"Been trying to reach you. Affirmative, I have overwatch on Poppa, alive but wounded. Four hostiles with him."

Darwin felt the relief flood him. Now he had something to work with, knowing it was still a rescue mission and not a recovery. He could tell this story with Gabe sitting next to him, shaking his head, instead of never talking about it again.

"Can you engage?"

"Negative," Cal said. "They're alert, one goes down they'll kill him. Think I know which one is in charge, keeps trying his cell phone, maybe running it up the chain to see what the hell he should do now."

"Where are they?"

"Tower site is twelve o'clock. They're at five, two ridge lines away from the river, about five hundred yards. I'm below the second ridge, closer to four o'clock. They're dug into a little bunker, camo netting on top and sandbags around it. Can't tell for sure, but they might have a cave entrance."

Not good. Darwin pictured the area from above, wasn't sure where his tunnel exit was, took an educated guess. "Check seven o'clock, watch for my light."

He sent the IR illuminator and aiming laser through the cave's mouth, waved it around.

"Got you," Cal said. "You're on the back side of the first ridge. I'm blind to what's around you though, can't say if you have company."

"Copy. Any sign of Robbie?"

"Negative."

"I'll sweep around six, approach Poppa from the southwest."

"I have overwatch on most of that."

"Moving," Darwin said, and took two steps before he had to stop, duck back against the cave wall and hold his breath.

The three men walking into the cave hadn't made any sound, their boots silent on the packed sand. Darwin wanted to kick himself, letting his guard down like that.

The men moved past him and didn't need any light to find the truck. One walked around to the driver's side and got in, no dome light inside the cab. The other two stepped on the back tire and into the truck bed. They each sat on a wheel well and rested their rifles across their thighs, started chatting.

Darwin had moved with them, slid along the pallets and used the near man's body to block the further's line of sight as they sat down. His Spanish was functional, not quite conversational, his time in Delta and since then mostly spent on Farsi and Arabic. The men in the truck were talking about the best spot for an execution, one of them saying if they were going to use gasoline to burn the prisoners alive, they should do it close to the river, see if the men tried to run for the water.

The driver said it wasn't up to them, kept talking while Darwin let the M4 hang from its sling, pulled the .45 and moved in toward the closest man's back. When the driver started the truck Darwin shot the furthest man in the face, reached up and hooked his forearm around the near man's chin, slammed it against his windpipe.

The man's hands came up away from his rifle. Darwin clamped the arm around his neck and tore him out of the truck bed, put the .45 in his choking hand for a second to open the passenger door, switched it back and put the long suppressor in the driver's face.

The driver stopped talking.

Darwin said in Spanish, "Where is Robbie?"

The man didn't move or say anything.

Darwin had seen the effect before, the shock of a faceless man armed to the teeth appearing from nowhere. He'd give him one more chance. The second man started to struggle, took one hand away from Darwin's arm and fumbled around his waist.

Darwin didn't wait to find out what he was reaching for. He dumped the man onto the ground, stepped on his chest and shot him in the head. Pointed the .45 at the driver again. "Where is Robbie?"

"I'm going to get him."

"Where?"

"The house. A house we use."

"To bring him back and execute him?"

The man closed his mouth.

"I heard you talking."

"Okay, yes, to kill him."

"How far?"

He shrugged. "An hour, to go and come back. I was going to get some food too."

"Who else is there?"

"Many soldiers," he said, puffing up.

Darwin got in and closed the door. "We'll see."

●●●

Cal saw headlights pop on and show the landscape down where Darwin was.

He touched his mic. "Vehicle."

"I'm inside it, don't engage," Darwin said, engine sounds nearby. "Going to get Robbie with—*Como se llamo?*—with Luis."

"Who is Luis?"

"You got overwatch on Gabe for an hour?"

"I can sit here all week, it's up to them what happens. They get jumpy I'll have to go for it."

"Can you approach?"

"Well sure, now I know you're joyriding. Say hello to Luis for me."

"He's busy."

Busy shitting his pants, Cal thought. He checked his gear, pouches, everything in place, and started working clockwise around the ridges and brush to come at the guys holding Gabe from their blind spot.

•••

Maro stood over Anna and made sure she was still breathing before he leaned further into the shipper, tried to identify who was standing right there in the blackness.

Marty said, "Jesus, Maro, did you kill her?"

"Not yet. Who's that with you?"

"Dave. Watch out, I think she has a couple Border agents out there with her."

"They chasing my guys, but the others are coming in from the arroyo. I need to scoot."

Marty stepped close and Maro could smell him, the stress and fear, the scent of a cornered animal. "Who's winning?"

"You keeping score?"

"I mean who's left?"

Maro said, "I don't know anybody's dead yet. We have one of your babysitters, so the other two are running around looking for him. They were going to the tunnel, so they probably dead by now." A shame, he thought. It would have felt good to be the one to kill Darwin. "And now I have Anna."

"You have her? What's that mean?"

"I'm taking her across the border, she gonna help me with my plan."

"Maro, we need to make sure these people can't report what they've seen here."

"Maybe."

"Maybe?" Marty looked over his shoulder at Dave, who was just a shape. "No maybes. We need to kill this bitch and the rest of the Border agents. I need plausible deniability."

"Come on, you talking crazy now. They'll know you working with the cartel. Of course they will."

Marty's face pinched, got tiny, then sagged. Now it's sunk in, Maro thought.

"Okay," Marty said. "Okay, we're coming with you. Get us across the border and to an airport."

"Who?"

"Me and Dave."

"You have more men in here."

"Fuck them," Marty said.

Maro pictured it, dragging the two of them across the river with Marty pissing and moaning the whole time, saying they should go this way instead. Then flying away, only to get extradited back to the U.S. and spill everything. That would be good, get the country angry, but they would be angry at Marty, not the cartels.

Either way, it wasn't worth listening to him any longer.

He shot Marty in the chest, a short burst from the AK that ripped his shirt apart and tossed him back toward Dave, who tried to catch him. Maro shot Dave too, sent bursts into both shapes until they were a dark heap on the floor.

He thought about the other men somewhere in the shipper, probably squeezed into balls with their hands over their ears. Give them something to tell the authorities.

"*Viva la sustantivo!*"

Wait, maybe they don't speak Spanish.

"*Viva la* cartels!"

He tossed Anna's weapons aside, scooped her up and got her over his shoulder with her round hip pressed against his ear, damn, heavier than she looked, and threaded his way into the scrub toward the Rio.

CHAPTER 18

DARWIN RODE WITH Luis in silence, his night optics off and flipped up on his helmet. He'd kept the .45 pointed at Luis's face until they got clear of the little base camp with its bunkers and caves, case the guy got clever and started honking the horn and flashing lights.

Now he leaned against the door with the .45 in his lap, still pointed in Luis's direction but not overt. The look on Luis's face told Darwin the guy was happy to take him to this house where all his friends were.

"Who else is at the house?" Darwin asked in Spanish.

"I tole you already," Luis said in English, his accent heavy.

"Hey, look at you. I didn't know you speak English."

"You don't ask."

Darwin ran through his radio conversation with Cal, made sure he hadn't given anything away. "You speak it well?"

"Better than your *Espanol*, my friend."

Fair enough. "So who's at the house, just the soldiers and Robbie?"

"Oh, no, more hostages too. Families of the workers." He bobbed in his seat and reached for the middle console to shift, the movement making Darwin edgy.

"Just leave your hand on the shifter."

"Okay."

"Where are the workers?"

"They in some of the caves. Not the one you saw, lucky them. They all be shot now."

Darwin said, "Is this a big house, where Robbie is?"

"Eh, more like a villa. A compound."

"And they know you're coming."

"Yes, Arturo called them."

"Who is Arturo?" Darwin said.

Luis winced, like he might get in trouble over putting the name out there. "You don't need to know all this, man. It's going to be over for you soon."

No use threatening him—Luis knew Darwin needed him to get to the house. "Is Arturo second in command to Maro?"

That made him look over and smile. "You know Maro."

"We've met."

"I'm surprised you still around."

"You think he'd scare me off?"

"Mostly kill you, but scare too, sure."

"Huh. What can you tell me about him?"

Luis gripped the steering wheel, shifted in his seat. "You killed my friends back there."

"Yes. You have my friend hostage. And Robbie. I want them back."

"Is too bad."

"Luis, do you understand what will happen if you murder these men?"

"I'm a soldier, following orders."

Jesus, Darwin thought. They came to the first crossroad, just another two-track cutting across the desert, and he marked the features as Luis turned right to head almost due west. In the side mirror Darwin saw the eastern skyline starting to glow.

"Maro doesn't look like he's from Mexico."

"He's Cubano," Luis said.

"Cartel thinks you can't handle this on your own?"

"He's a specialist, so they brought him in to work with

your friend Martin."

"Not my friend. A specialist in what?"

Luis shrugged. "Being crazy? Sleeping under rocks. It works though, we been back and forth across your border so many times already."

"You like him as a boss, telling you what to do?"

Luis looked over. "You not getting to me, man. He's only in charge because the cartel says it's so, that's it. We get to the house, you meet the guys who can say it's time to kill Maro and guess what? I go back and kill him."

"Why would they say that?"

"I don't know if they will, I'm saying they can. It's up to them, not Maro. He's not my boss."

"Well Luis, this Cuban that isn't your boss is getting you all killed."

●●●

Maro was almost to the river, the gunfire between his *salvajes* and the two men who had abandoned Anna somewhere behind him when he heard the helicopter coming, probably equipped with forward-looking infrared and spotlights. He was far upstream from the sunken bridge but knew where he was along the river and decided to go for it, Anna's dead weight bouncing up and down and killing his shoulder.

He crashed into the brush along the riverbank, saw the dark stripe of the drop-off ahead. He stopped at the edge, knelt and tipped sideways to let Anna slide off into the dirt, then he jumped down onto the damp mud and saw that yes, he was at the stretch of river where it had carved out an overhang when it was running high and fast.

Maro pulled Anna over the edge and shoved her into the

roots and silt and got in with her, a good two or three feet of earth above them. The helicopter got louder, reminded him a bit of the Russian Hinds in Afghanistan but a different sound to the rotor. It swept close above him and peeled away to the northwest, toward his *salvajes* who were still shooting, maybe, but it was hard to tell with the helicopter making so much noise.

He checked on Anna. Her eyes were squeezed shut, not relaxed, but her breathing seemed okay. He felt the back of her skull. Some tacky blood there, but no loose bone shards or anything that felt like her brain was swelling.

Be honest. She could be dying, you wouldn't know.

Well, she hasn't pissed herself yet. His men and enemies on the battlefield, when they started messing their pants, it was usually a matter of time.

So she wasn't dying, he didn't think, but she was dead weight. He didn't want to swim with her across the river. It was close to fifty feet wide here and swift. Maybe the current would take them through the twists and turns between here and the sunken bridge, wash them up on it and let him carry her across, but it could also pull them under into the pipes Marty's men had buried. Suck them in and spit them out the other end, maybe alive but probably not.

That was more likely. And the brush was too thick along the bank to get to the bridge that way.

You're stuck, just relax and don't worry about it.

He pulled his cell phone out, powered it up and called Arturo.

"We hear a helicopter," Arturo said. Low, like the helicopter could hear him too.

"Yes, it's above me."

"You're caught?"

"Who said that? I'm safe. I have Anna, the Border agent."

"What for?"

What for? "To kill with the others, Robbie and the one you have. What's his name?"

"He won't say. How rough can we get?"

"Don't bother. If he isn't Darwin it doesn't matter. Is he going to live for a while?"

"He got shot up along his neck, took off part of his ear. He's fine."

"Has everyone checked in?"

Arturo said, "I was hoping they did with you."

"No, I told you, I need to be loose tonight, no chains. Who hasn't checked in?"

"Angel, with the cavemen, and Luis. But I told Luis to go get Robbie, so maybe he's just busy."

Maro was quiet. The men in the tunnel hadn't checked in, and neither had the one who'd gone to the safe house. The problem with some of these men—were they just being undisciplined, or were they dead? It would be a relief when he didn't have to worry about it anymore.

Arturo said, "I was going to tell you right away, but the helicopter had me worried."

"Where are you?"

"Bunker seven."

"They won't see you. Even if they do, what can they do? But listen, I think Darwin and the other one are hunting you."

"We have men watching. And we're staying close to this one, I don't think anyone would risk a shot."

"I need you to bring him to the river so everyone can see him die."

"Now?"

"No," Maro said, "I need to cross. I'll let you know. Hold on." He was thinking and talking, had to stay quiet to look hard at his idea. "Okay, you need to take him to the back of the bunker, into the cave."

It wasn't much of a cave, just a scoop into the rocks that was a good place to sit when the sun was too hot. He heard Arturo telling the men to do it.

"Okay, he's there."

Maro said, "I don't think you're going to like the next part."

Anna twitched, moaned something. Maro talked fast, told Arturo what to do.

Arturo was silent, then said, "You're right, I don't like it."

"But you'll do it."

"Of course."

"My soldier."

Maro turned the phone off and listened for the helicopter, far away to the north. He put the phone in a cloudy plastic baggie and wrapped it up, stowed it in a pouch. He took a few steps to the water and came back with his hands cupped, tossed the water onto Anna's face to wake her up so she could see her last sunrise.

● ● ●

Cal had to break visual contact with the bunker to work his way around its blind side and come at it from about three o'clock, moving low through the loose rocks and cactus, not much cover.

The growing daylight was taking away his night optics advantage—anybody standing out here in the dark would have eyes better adjusted than his. He killed the optics and flipped them up, tried to block out the sound of the helo across the river and listen to the area around him.

Even the bugs were quiet over here, not sure what to think of all the racket. Cal took a step toward a jumble of big rocks fifteen feet away, the last real cover between him and the ridge that looked down on the bunker, when one of the rocks shifted and stood up, turned into a man wrapped in some kind of blanket with an assault rifle in his hands.

Cal froze, held the guy in his peripheral vision so he could see him better in the dark and to keep him from feeling eyes on him, go red alert. The man was straight ahead, his right shoulder pointed at Cal. He stretched his legs and looked at the helo zipping around over US soil.

Shit. Close as they were to the bunker, even the suppressed weapons would be too loud. And who else is out here? Christ, almost stepped on that one, great work. The guy's feet don't fall asleep, you would have leaned right against him.

He'd tell Darwin and Gabe about it later, but he was glad they weren't here to see it.

The guy stood on his tiptoes, arched his back and grunted. Shook a leg out. Turned a little to his left, toward the bunker down the slope from him that Cal still couldn't see.

He was left-handed, the barrel of the rifle pointing to Cal's right.

Then he whistled, seemed to wait for something, and whistled again. Said in Spanish, "Hey, I need to piss. Bring him up here to catch it for me."

Somebody stage-whispered back, "Shut the fuck up."

The man laughed. The helo banked and sent a louder chop at them from across the Rio and Cal knew he wouldn't get a better chance.

Dammit.

He took a breath and left the sniper rifle behind, slid the five-inch dagger out of its sheath on his chest rig and reverse-gripped it in his left hand, the point toward the ground. He moved as fast as he could toward the man, two steps and he was on him, wrapped his right forearm around his throat and pulled him backward, hooked the blade into the crook of the man's left arm and ripped it away from the rifle. Cal yanked him backward, dropped with him, Cal's feet shooting back so he landed on his stomach and the man landed on his back.

He kept the man's throat clamped and drove his right

shoulder forward into the back of his head, leaned into it with his two-hundred forty pounds until he was looking over the guy's left shoulder, all sorts of things popping in the guy's neck. Cal brought the blade down in a tight arc, punched it into the man's chest and scrambled it around, slicing the heart, kept it there until the man went slack.

Cal pulled the blanket loose, a large burlap sack that was perfect camouflage for this landscape but itchy as hell, wiped his blade clean and draped the burlap over the body. Went back for the sniper rifle, listened—no alarms going off—and eased up to the ridge again.

Now he wanted the sun higher, blinding anybody looking up toward the ridge. Until then he'd be a big fat-headed silhouette.

He tilted his head and poked one eye over, saw the bunker about thirty yards below on an angle. He could see into a gap between the camo netting and sandbags, empty soda cans and water bottles scattered on the dirt floor.

No people.

●●●

Darwin saw the buildings ahead, one- and two-story squares with flat roofs and lights in some of the windows. The sun hadn't topped the ridges behind the truck yet, but morning was here. The two-track they were on bounced them down a hill into a junkyard on the edge of the little village. Luis downshifted and wove between burnt cars, appliances with bullet holes, heaps of rusted fencing.

Darwin pointed the .45 in his right hand at Luis, had switched the M4 to his left and had the barrel resting on the windowsill. He'd stowed the IR sight and night optics, reattached the ACOG. He scanned the piles of junk, all the shadows and perfect spots to hide. A shape moved, turned into a dog that gave Darwin a worried look and trotted away.

Darwin said, "This how you usually come in?"

"Yes."

"Not some route you only use if you're in trouble."

Luis shrugged. "We never talked about it. Why would we be in trouble here?"

"Where's the house?"

"The middle of town."

"Any checkpoints, guards we need to get past?"

"I told you man, this is our place. You gonna see." He smiled. "Hey, you show me how to use those goggles you have? I want them after they boys take care of you."

"Luis. I thought we were friends."

"Sure. I seen lots of friends die, no big deal."

Darwin kept his eyes sweeping. He could see a couple dozen structures on this side of the village, adobes and shacks and lean-tos, the higher roofs further on toward the center. Far off to the right there was a group of people walking away into the desert with buckets. Overall there were more buildings than he'd expected, certainly more people. How many of them had guns and would want to kill him—well, one was too many.

He said, "Now that your little tunnel project is over, you should know Robbie is worth more alive than dead. So whatever happens to me, you should keep him safe."

"Is not up to me."

"Then you tell whoever you need to. Robbie is a valuable bargaining chip. The United States will want him back. The Border agents are already working on it."

"Okay. And to get him they send, what, money? Gold? Nah. I think they send more men like you."

"Better than me," Darwin said. "But you can play it smart, avoid having to meet them some night."

Luis honked the horn, a quick bleat that pulled Darwin's head around.

"The fuck you doing?"

Luis was grinning, staring right back at him. "I need to do that, tell the boys I'm coming in."

Darwin raised the .45 to Luis's face. "Do not fuck with me."

He honked again, a longer blast, and sped up the hill toward the houses. There was a glint in his eyes, a new hardness that looked like a challenge.

"Luis. If you're bringing them down on me, you die first."

The truck bounced across a ditch and rolled between two houses, the wall close enough the side mirrors almost scraped the faded paint. Darwin saw too late what Luis was doing, cursed and braced himself against the dashboard just as Luis stomped the brake.

The truck skidded to a halt between the houses, an alley so narrow neither of the truck doors could open.

"Go," Darwin said.

Luis turned the truck off, pulled the keys and dropped them out his window. "I think we wait here." He turned and put his back against his door, looked at Darwin with no fear. "You shoot me, man, it's better than the deaths I imagined. I'm gonna get killed by this cartel or another one, and guns too quick for them. So shoot, do me a favor."

Darwin called himself a fucking idiot and checked the side and rear windows—not enough room. The windshield would take a lot of noise and work.

Luis put his elbow on the horn, leaned onto it and kept it going. More lights popped on in the houses across the narrow street in front of them. Luis raised his voice: "This gonna be good. They come around the corner and see me and you in here."

Darwin shot him in the face with the .45, sprayed the back of his head across the wall behind him. Luis's elbow came off the horn. Darwin opened his door six inches before it hit the wall. He shut it, saw Luis's was even closer to the house over there. Darwin put his left foot over the console and pushed the clutch to the floor, knocked the truck into neutral and held his breath.

Nothing.

"Fuck." He leaned against dashboard, drove back and slammed his shoulder into the seat. The truck rocked once, stayed where it was. He tried again, got the same thing.

A man shouted something from the other side of the houses in front of him, a question. Another man answered from somewhere to Darwin's right, around the corner where he couldn't see. He shoved the .45 in its holster and set the M4 barrel on top of the side mirror, which showed the corner behind him.

"Godammit." Someone comes around there, this truck is your coffin.

He slammed back into the seat again, again, kept going until he saw the house start to slide forward. He turned in the seat and reached out his window, stuck his fingers in a crack in the wall of the house and pulled, yelled through his teeth and kept the truck going.

When it rolled back from between the houses Darwin was out his door and moving. He ran past four houses before he ducked into an empty lean-to, stopped and listened, more men yelling now and engines starting.

The truck bumped through the ditch and rolled back into the junkyard, Luis's body flopping around until it fell across the seat and disappeared, a hand flailing up once more when the truck hit a pile of broken concrete and stopped.

A man stepped through the opening where the truck had been, showing Darwin his left profile. Darwin put the man's face behind the red dot in the ACOG, waited. The man didn't look left or right, just yelled down to the truck, frowned, and walked down the hill.

Darwin turned and moved through the lean-to toward the center of the village.

CHAPTER 19

IT WAS STILL chilly under the muddy overhang. Maro looked out at the river in full sun, just a few meters away, but not a spot he could enjoy just yet. Anna was shivering but wouldn't take his suggestions to get up and move around a little, just stay under his little roof.

He tried again: "You want to warm up before we get in the water."

She didn't say anything, just stared at his boots. Like she was waiting for him to make the wrong move, give her the chance to do something stupid. The helicopter was still skimming around up the hill, spending a lot of time beyond the tower site if his ears were right. Where his *salvajes* had moved in to pull the Border agents away from the arroyo.

So there was something there to see.

"Did any of your men get killed?" he asked.

"No. Did yours?"

Now she talks. She had a red bump on her jaw where he'd punched her. It would turn into a good bruise if they didn't get across the water soon.

He said, "Don't you consider Marty one of your men? Dave?"

She opened her mouth, then her eyebrows came together and she put both hands on her head. "Wait. You shot somebody up there."

He patted the *saperka*. "You were on the ground."

"You shot Marty."

He gave her a wink.

"You're under arrest."

That one caught him off guard, made him laugh and cover his mouth with the back of his wrist. "Sorry. Okay, I'm your prisoner. Here's my gun."

He pointed it at her face, winked again while she held her breath. He set the rifle across his thighs. "That helicopter has to leave soon. Unless you have the ones that don't need fuel to stay in the air, you have those yet?"

He raised his eyebrows at her, see if she'd play along. She wasn't even looking at him.

"Will another one come to take its place, or will it have to hurry to the gas station and back? Anna, you should tell me. The more I know, the less I worry. When I worry I have to do things fast, hard, make sure they happen. You know?"

She was looking at her boots again. No, wait. At the rocks sticking out of the mud near her boots, some of them a little bigger than a baseball. Small enough to grab and throw or club him with. Her hands were curled against her stomach, folded up in the sleeves and bulk of her jacket.

He could smash her fingers with the rifle butt, or chop them off with the *saperka*. But he needed her to be able to swim. Maybe one hand. She didn't know he couldn't do them both.

"Put your hands flat on the ground."

"They're cold."

"Do what I say."

"Go fuck yourself."

Maro grabbed her sleeve and yanked her arm toward him, all of it coming too easily. Her sleeve was empty. He saw her hand come out the bottom of her jacket and grab a rock, pluck it out of the mud. Her face was twisted, teeth showing and eyes wide.

He pulled his head back but not far enough. She swung the rock in an uppercut that clunked into his jaw and made him bite his tongue, might have knocked him out if her jacket hadn't bunched up and restricted her arm movement.

She swung her other fist at him, slipped in the mud and missed by at least a foot, fell against the slope. He liked that she was able to move now, not a lump he'd have to drag around. Her jacket was up around her neck. She jerked it down and tried to find the zipper, blinked and tipped almost onto her back.

"Your head still fuzzy?" Maro said. "I gave you a good smack."

She still had the rock in her right hand, cocked up near her ear.

He saw her weight shift, getting ready, so he put his boot on her wrist. "Okay, settle down. This is to make sure we get along from now on."

He pulled the *saperka* out of its sheath. She made a growling noise and kicked him in the back, tried to get her boot against him to shove him away.

"Anna, stop it. Calm down."

He lifted the *saperka* to his shoulder, not much of a swing needed to take the fingers as long as he followed through into the mud underneath. He stopped, froze there.

The helicopter was getting quieter.

Looping around?

No, leaving.

Anna kicked him again.

"Behave." He spun the *saperka* and thumped the flat side against her head, just a tap, but her brain was having a hard day. She went limp.

Maro cursed and put the *saperka* away, hauled Anna onto his shoulder and walked into the Rio.

●●●

Cal could hear sounds coming out of the bunker below him. Thumps and grunts but no screaming or talking. Almost sounded like an interrogation, but there weren't any questions being asked, far as he could tell.

He was tucked under some scrub on the other side of the slope from the man's body under the burlap, which was gathering flies already. He wanted to keep moving, work clockwise around the hill to get a peek into the bunker, but once he could actually see into it he'd be staring into the sun still taking its time getting up there.

Gabe was right underneath him, maybe getting worked over, and what could he do?

Storm it. He'd seen four or five guys standing there with Gabe. If they were the only ones in there, speed, surprise, and violence of action ought to be enough. More than that, or if they have a gun on Gabe, things could get unreasonable.

Say it does work, then what? Drag Gabe back over the hills, who knows how many hostiles pouring out of the caves like fire ants. Fight across the Rio and get a call from Darwin saying they killed the Robbie guy because of all the racket.

Shit, maybe he could flag that helo. He didn't have any smoke or flares. And it probably wasn't allowed to cross the border.

There was a loud smack from the bunker, then somebody laughed.

Cal pictured them knocking Gabe around, having a good time while his friend suffered, no idea how to handle it. Gabe never had the survival, evade, resistance, escape training he and Darwin had, or any kind of S.E.R.E. experience, unless they taught it at the Detroit Metro Police Department. Shit, maybe they did. Cal had a strong need to ask Gabe about it, that and all kinds of things they'd never discussed.

He pushed it away, focused. His beard itched, made him even grumpier. He tried the radio, tapped his throat mic once and waited for Darwin to come back.

Nothing.

The repeater was sitting in their trailer, meant to keep the radios working for line-of-sight communications around the tower area. A nice surprise they'd worked on this side of the river at all. Cal pulled out his cell phone. It had a decent signal.

He listened to a few more thumps before he thought, Fuck it, hit the Call button and hoped Darwin had his phone on vibrate.

●●●

Darwin was in what had to be an abandoned house, chicken and goat shit all over the floor, everything covered in a layer of dust and fine sand. He was crouched next to a glassless window looking at the building in the center of town, a square structure about fifty feet on each side from what he could see.

It looked like it had started out as a church. Three stories, white stucco walls and a red tiled roof with a spire in the center. There was a low wall framing the building and some grass, was meant to be decorative but now had sandbags stacked on top with machine gun emplacements at each corner.

No machine guns that he could see, but those were the worst kind. The church windows were covered with scraps of sheet metal, car hoods, ragged lumber, slits in every one that would let anybody in there shoot at him with relative safety.

Well, this was some bullshit right here.

He leaned right and checked to his left down the street,

could see the group of men still standing there with AKs and AR-15s, holding them like tools they were used to operating.

The gate into the church square was around that corner—he could see the top of it over the wall closest to him—but he wasn't going near that thing unless a couple dozen Rangers showed up with some Humvees.

His cell phone vibrated in the thigh pouch. Darwin stepped back into the shadows and noticed his knees really complaining for the first time since he'd put Marty in the shipper. Don't start with me, he told them, got his phone out and thought it might be Christine calling about the divorce, some real perspective, saw it was Cal.

He kept his voice low and covered his mouth and the phone with a hand, kept the M4 pointed at the window in case any faces popped through. "Sheepdog."

"Sheep, Nilla." Cal was whispering too. "Status?"

"Believe I have Robbie's location in sight. Absolutely no idea how I'm gonna get him out."

"Green light to take Gabe back?"

"You have the shot?"

"Gotta kick a door in, kinda, but he's close by. Not a sure thing."

"Can it wait?" Darwin said.

"They're working on him. It's time to move. I'm waiting to hear the shot, the one tells me they're tired of it and I get to replay the rest of my life, over and over."

"Okay. I'm still working here, but go get him. Green light."

●●●

Maro pulled Anna across the Rio, all her clothes and gear pulling them both under. His rifle and things were heavy too, but he was used to them, just part of his body. His head kept bobbing below the water, too silty to see through, and pushing to keep Anna afloat only made him sink more.

Let her go, you have the babysitter with Arturo. He's enough.

Maybe enough, this needs more than that.

Wars don't start because of enough—they start because of too much.

The current sped up and carried them into a bend in the river that curled toward the US side, making a little peninsula of Mexico right in his path. He put everything into it, thrashed and kicked against the current and kept them from sweeping around the bend. When his boot kicked soft mud he gave a shout of triumph, then turned to make sure no one was standing on the US shore taking aim at him.

All clear.

He dropped Anna onto the Mexican shore and dragged her into the scrub, then spent a few minutes breathing hard and draining water out of his rifle even though he'd put it through worse many times and had no trouble. If things went right, his next shot could be very dramatic—to have it misfire would be embarrassing.

Anna was pale with dark lips and circles under eyes, but she was breathing. All that work to keep her alive, just to shoot her or chop her with the *saperka* when the time was right.

Man, you making this happen.

He debated what to do next, decided it was the professional thing to do and got his phone out. He called Rojo, the man in charge of the church and village the Luna Cartel had pretty much taken over.

"I was just about to call you," Rojo said.

"Yes?"

"What the fuck is going on out there?"

Maro could hear men yelling and engines speeding on the other end. Did Arturo say too much? "Why, what have you heard?"

"Nothing, but Luis is here, dead in one of your trucks. Somebody shot him in the face."

"Stop it."

Rojo yelled at someone away from the phone, came back. "Tell me what's happening."

"You're sure he didn't shoot himself by accident? Or he was depressed?"

"Yes, he shot himself and threw the gun away where we can't find it, then he died."

Maro stared at the sand and rocks between his boots, tried to work through this thing he hadn't considered for even a second until now. "Okay, you have at least one, maybe two US Special Forces operators inside the village."

"The hell you saying?"

"They're from here, the tower site, the security men and they're coming for the engineer. Robbie."

Rojo was quiet for a moment. "How do they know about him? Wait, how did they get past you?"

"I'll tell you later. What I'm going to do is kill a Border agent and another one of the security men on the shore of the Rio. Robbie too, if you can get him here quickly. It's time to stop playing at this and get serious."

This time Rojo was silent long enough that Maro thought the call had been cut off, then he said, "Maro, listen to me. That is a very bad idea. Do not do it."

"It's already happening. I have the agent right here, a woman named Anna. She would say hello but she's unconscious."

"I'm coming to you. Don't do anything until I get there."

"Sure, coming to stop me. This is the right thing, Rojo. This is what men like you and me are made for. Well, me anyway. We'll see about you. Good luck with the Americans."

He turned the phone off, looked at Anna breathing through the spittle around her mouth, her eyes twitching behind the lids. "Our friend Darwin has invaded Mexico.

Him or the one with the beard, maybe both, but it's Darwin calling the shots. I liked him before, but this impresses me. You know what? I want him to beat Rojo. Rojo isn't worthy. I hope me and the Sheepdog get a chance to find out who's the better soldier, but I'm afraid it won't happen. If he's the one at the church, they gonna have a nasty surprise ready for him."

CHAPTER 20

CAL WAS WRAPPED in the burlap he'd pulled off the dead sentry, had it up over his head and draped down to cover most of his face. He was working down the slope to the far side of the cave opening to come at it with his shadow behind him.

The M4 was under the burlap too, hanging from his chest sling with a finger on the trigger. He walked like a man pissed about having to stand out in the dark all night, waiting for something to happen and getting nothing. The corner of the opening was about twenty feet away. He could see the sandbags and camo netting but not what was inside the cave.

He played it through like it had already happened:

Into the opening. Gabe is in the back on the floor. Five men standing around him. One turns, yells at Cal to get back up to his post.

Assess. Release the burlap and come out of it with the M4 up, a burst into the man looking at him. Two into the man closest to Gabe and work his way out, drop them all.

Maybe one and a half seconds from the first shot to the last.

Haul Gabe up and get moving.

Cal was ten feet from the entrance when four men came out carrying Gabe. Cal melted into the slope and held his breath. Gabe was up on their shoulders, face-down. Not moving, impossible to tell if he was alive but he didn't have the dead-weight look of a corpse.

Two of the men had their heads on either side of Gabe's with his arms around their necks. The third had Gabe's knees on his shoulders, his head tucked to see where he was stepping. The fourth duck-walked under Gabe's belly, his rifle pointed at Gabe's face.

One of the men in the front shouted over his shoulder to the dead man above the cave, told him to stay there and watch for anybody closing in on them. They were going to the river.

Cal looked for any kind of shot. Boys were positioned to beat a sniper, their heads and bodies close to or blocked by Gabe's. At close range though—get in and take out the one in the middle, then the tailgunner before the other two.

He'd need a broadside shot, willed them to turn left and present it to him but they turned right, on a line straight away, showing him the bottom of Gabe's boots. They were on a trail that curled counter-clockwise around a hill straight ahead of the bunker, curled down to the cave where Darwin had come out. That was as far as he could see when he'd been on top of the bunker, but from there it made sense that the trail would cut around that peak, over the ridge and down to the Rio.

They moved slowly, the duck-walker setting the pace. Cal waited until they were around the hill. He ditched the burlap and moved into the cave, had to clear it before he moved on.

It went into the hillside about thirty feet, nobody inside. There were crates and shrink-wrapped flats of bottled water stacked along the back wall, more empties piled against the sides. He could smell fresh blood and old sweat.

Cal knelt in the mouth of the cave, saw no one, and sprinted down the slope toward the hill. Started up, fast but careful not to make any noise. Figured the closer he got to the

Rio, the more guys he'd have to worry about.

So get to the top and look down on Gabe and the assholes. Long as no one else is around, take them down. Best chance you're gonna get.

He got close to the top and moved to a belly crawl, cursed the sun behind him and eased his eyes over.

Fuck me, he thought.

•••

Darwin was still in the abandoned house, and from what he could see none of the structures around him were occupied by families or normal citizens. The people coming out were either cartel gunmen or forced labor. The laborers, men and women, would turn around and go back inside after a look at the commotion; the gunmen would run toward the church.

About two dozen of the latter.

So far.

They ran up to a Mexican guy—older than the rest, Darwin put him around forty—standing at the corner of the church wall. He had two cell phones going and would pull them away from his mouth to tell the gunmen something.

Off they went, some into the church, others fanning out into the village until the man with the phones yelled at them, got them into a group and pointed at one of the houses. They broke into four groups. Three ran through alleys and out of Darwin's line of sight.

The last group stacked up in a sloppy line outside a house and stormed it, came out a few seconds later. Not a large house. They moved to the next one, toward Darwin's.

He moved closer to the window, looked along the dirt road and saw there were maybe twenty houses before they got to his. Had to assume the other two groups were doing the same to the outer tiers.

Darwin moved away from the window. They keep the current pace, you got about three minutes.

Or hole up, let them pass.

Okay, where? Under that pile of bricks? And then what, just in case they don't find you and shoot you while you're hiding?

"Shit."

He checked the window again, heard engines getting louder. Two vehicles slid to a stop next to the phone man— hey, one of them the Jeep they'd seen on the way to the job site—more guys riding in the back with assault rifles pointed at the sky.

The house clearers had gone through five so far. Laborers were tossed into the street and shoved to kneel against the outside of the houses, faces pressed to the walls. Another engine, this one familiar, then the truck he and Luis had used rolled up to the phone man and stopped.

The phone man opened the passenger door. Darwin watched Luis's head and torso flop out, the phone man looking down at it then sweeping one hand away. A gunman ran up and yanked the body out to land in the dust. The phone man leaned inside the truck, his full back to Darwin.

Somalia, Afghanistan, Croatia, Iraq, Darfur—didn't matter where, there was always some asshole with a cell phone bossing everybody around. In Delta, Darwin and his team had referred to them as The Infrastructure.

Hundred yards. Cake shot.

Darwin put the red dot between the man's shoulder blades. Took a breath, let half out and held the rest.

If the guys around him were sharp, they'd know which direction the shot came from.

They're coming this way already.

Guessing. Not targeting.

Darwin lowered his rifle and breathed.

The phone man yelled at the vehicles. One slewed around

and took off along the road Darwin wasn't on. He could see the dust rolling up above the church wall. The Jeep roared straight down his road. Maybe to flush him out, maybe to set up a perimeter.

Shit, maybe headed for the Rio to shoot at Cal.

The house clearers were close enough that Darwin couldn't see them anymore, even when he pressed the right side of his helmet against the wall a few feet away from the window.

He stayed there, tight to the wall, and let the Jeep shoot past. Then he couldn't see anything with the dust pouring through the window, knew this was the only chance he was going to get.

He stepped through the window and sprinted into the dust cloud, counted his steps and anticipated the church wall, jumped before he could see it. His knee buckled as he pushed off, tipped him into a stumble until he hit the four-foot wall and two feet of sandbags on top.

"Motherfuck."

The dust was clearing. Darwin scrambled up the wall, got his forearms on top and stuck his boot in a crevice, levered over and dropped. It was only a four-foot drop, the ground inside built up to allow the men defending the church to lean over the sandbags.

Dust rolled over the wall above him and drifted down, hid his view of the church. The Jeep engine faded and he could hear men across the street going into a house, maybe his. Darwin kept still. He was on his belly, the M4 under him.

When the dust cleared he saw a man fifteen feet away staring right at him with a pistol in his hand.

●●●

Cal watched them carry Gabe along the trail, curving in front of him and then away, down the slope toward the cave entrance Darwin had come out of.

He counted eight men spread out on the hillsides along the trail, each one armed and facing the landscape, running a secure corridor for their package. Give him an hour and an assault team, two sniper teams, he could pull Gabe out with satisfactory confidence.

Or Gabe's body—he still didn't know.

Be a good time for the Sheepdog to come back in, pull some eyes away, maybe move into these guys from another angle so they could both close in on Gabe in a V.

Cal was looking for any other options when one of Gabe's leg bent, his boot coming up to touch the tailgunner in the head. Not nearly hard enough, but a sign of life. Cal retraced his steps to the top of the bunker, moving fast and low, weaving between scrub and rocks. He got behind the rifle and scanned the security detail—no hubbub or sign they'd spotted him.

The group carrying Gabe was close to the cave. The rangefinder in the scope put them at three hundred seventy yards. Cal could see a few feet of the cave's far wall, the rest cut off by the near side of the entrance. They stopped outside the cave.

They take Gabe inside, shit, what then?

Run back across and come at them the way Darwin had, through the tunnel.

Yeah, they'll sit tight for a few hours while you do that. Take your time. And Border and whoever else is on-scene won't mind.

The duck-walker came out from under Gabe and stepped into the cave, his AK ready. Something in there had him spooked.

Sheepdog leave you guys a little present?

The guy came back out, yelled to the security men nearest

him. They passed it along, Cal straining to pick it up but just hearing sounds, not words. Put them on red alert, whatever it was.

The security corridor started moving, sliding along the landscape to keep pace with the group carrying Gabe. They were hustling now, bouncing him around at double-time past the cave and around the hill, on a trail that had to take them to the Rio.

Cal packed up and moved, sprinted down the back side of the bunker and started up the ridge, the features different now in daylight but some things familiar from his nighttime approach. He cut away from his insertion path, up toward the peak to keep an eye on Gabe while me moved. The cartel boys looked like they had a purpose, somewhere to be, but if they gave him a chance he'd put them all down.

●●●

Darwin and the man with the pistol stared at each other for what seemed like ten minutes—was actually less than a second—flashes of information playing through Darwin's head.

M4 is pinned, facing the wall.

Roll toward the pistol, under his shot and fire from your back.

Too long.

As he was thinking his right hand swept to the thigh holster and pulled the .45, Darwin knowing the sound would be too loud even with the suppressor. It would bring the village down on him.

All this while the man was raising his pistol, pointing it and squeezing.

Water spat out of the hose. Fat drops smacked Darwin in

the face and knocked against his helmet.

"Be still," the man said in Spanish.

Darwin had the .45 on him now, hesitating, knowing that was a good way to get killed. He'd landed in an irrigation ditch surrounding a small garden. There were knee-high tomato plants between him and the man with the hose. Some corn. He couldn't identify any of the other plants.

The man looked about fifty, short and lean with a trimmed mustache. He switched the spray to a fine mist and moved it to water the plants near Darwin's head, bent down and looked at a large leaf with chunks chewed out of it. "How many are with you?"

"None. Just me."

The man gave him a crazy look, eyebrows pulled together, then shook his head. "Just one. Please don't point that at me."

Darwin lowered the .45 but kept it handy. "I'm looking for, ah, Roberto."

"Robbie?" He said it in English with a rolled R.

"Yes."

"What about the rest of us?"

Be nice. "I didn't know you were here."

"And now?" He plucked withered leaves off a plant and tossed them aside.

Darwin didn't know what to say, but the two words that had been spinning in his head finally stopped, forced him to give a good hard look: International Incident.

He'd almost killed this man, had already killed Mexican citizens. Whether Mexico wanted them as citizens was beside the point.

He was an invader.

Darwin pushed it away, a good topic for discussion when survival was established, and said, "I'll see what I can do."

"I know what you can do. They have guns inside."

The church loomed behind the man, twenty yards away at Darwin's three o'clock. It was on a little hill, good for the defenders and terrible for him; the slope would expose him to anybody on the other side of the wall. Take an angle to the right, go around the back and regroup.

There was a little orchard behind the church, not nearly enough concealment, let alone cover, but it would block him from anybody on the other side of the wall that ran along the back side.

Just get through twenty yards of open ground, uphill, gunmen all around. The slits in the boarded windows waited for him to try it.

Darwin heard a truck somewhere—there, out by the gate over the man's right shoulder. The mist from the hose made a veil, but through it he saw reflections off chrome and glass, the colors of the truck he'd shared with Luis. It pulled through the gate and rolled toward the church, stopped about forty yards away from Darwin at his one o'clock.

"Shut that off, I can't see."

"Neither can they."

Shit, the guy was hiding him.

A truck door slammed. Through the mist Darwin saw the shape of the phone man, the one in charge. He had a phone to his ear and walked fast toward the church, turned and came toward the garden. Darwin cleared the M4, got it pointed in that direction and sucked himself toward the earth.

The phone man shouted, "Hey, get back inside."

Darwin's man kept the water going. "Your boys are getting dust all over the plants."

"Fuck your plants, get inside!"

"Do you want to eat?"

"You want to get shot? If you're going to stay outside, get over here and wash out the truck before you die."

His shape turned and disappeared around the corner of the church.

The man bent and pulled more leaves. "That's Rojo, the boss. He's very dramatic."

"What's your name?"

"Oh, Hermán." He moved to shake, realized they both

had their hands full. He grinned, a full set of good teeth.

"Later," Darwin said. "Is Robbie in the church?"

"Yes. Like the guns."

"You mentioned those. You want the guns, Hermán?"

"We're tired of these animals." He swept the water back and forth. "They have my son at the Rio Bravo, digging their tunnel."

"The Grande?"

"Same thing."

Darwin said, "That tunnel won't be around much longer."

"So the time is right, yes? We don't have a way to get the guns, but you can help."

"You know how to use them?"

"Unfortunately."

Darwin heard men yelling on the other side of the wall, wood splintering, engines growling. "You get me into that church, I'll get them for you."

"Ready?"

CHAPTER 21

MARO CARRIED ANNA over his left shoulder to give the right one a break, also so he could keep the AK ready in case he bumped into Darwin or the beard. Maybe they were both at the church with Rojo, but he doubted it. They were the no-man-left-behind type, all of them gonna get killed trying to save one.

Or three, you count Robbie and Anna. But they didn't know about her yet, might never know. See her in heaven or whatever, frown and say, "What are you doing here?"

She was lighter with her coat and body armor stripped off, but still a load to be hauling through the brush all the way to the rendezvous. No way was he going to call Arturo and have him send *salvajes* to help. Arturo was busy, and the *salvajes* would see Anna and go crazy, their blood up from fighting.

He stepped over a bone-dry mesquite trunk lying in the dirt, decided if the boys he'd crossed the river with during the night—the ones who'd shot at the Border agents to pull them away from Marty and Anna—if they made it over and found Maro, he'd tell them to carry her.

Then it would be an order, not a request.

The helicopter wasn't back yet and he didn't hear any shooting. Pretty soon the agents who were still alive would figure out Anna was gone, then things would pick up.

Maro walked faster—he and Anna had to be in place when everybody showed up.

●●●

Darwin couldn't see anything.

He was curled up under some rough burlap sacks in Hermán's garden cart, two wheels with a wooden platform and sides, Hermán tilting and pushing it toward the church with two handles like a backward rickshaw. That made him think of Anna, Anna Ricks.

Don't call her now, you're a little busy.

Besides, she probably doesn't want to talk to you, all the shit you're pulling in her jurisdiction. Nah. Next time you see her, she'll have a lot to say. Start out with, "You have the right to remain silent."

Hermán was singing softly to himself, something about a saint, and in the same tune said, "At the corner."

The light outside the burlap changed. They were in shade now on the back side of the church. The cart bumped and squeaked, then stopped and leveled out. Hermán kept singing. Darwin was concerned, the guy possibly attracting attention for singing at a time like this, but maybe this was normal for the village.

Or Hermán.

The burlap came off and he was looking at the underside of a lean-to roof, garden tools hanging on the wall above him.

"It's safe," Hermán sang.

Darwin stuck an eye over the top of the cart, saw the orchard between him and the wall. Patches of the houses showed through. He couldn't see anybody moving out there, good chance they couldn't see him.

He eased out of the cart and stepped the way they'd come, checked the corner. Men still going house-to-house on the other side of the garden and wall, no one coming his way.

Hermán pulled the hose and sprayer out of the cart and hung them up. "If they finds my tools left out," he sang, "they will know I'm not well."

Darwin checked the other corner. Double-doors into the church, closed. Boarded windows past that.

He whispered, "How many inside?"

Hermán held up five fingers, looked at the weathered ceiling, changed it to six, seven. Then he shrugged.

Darwin pointed at the first floor, then the second floor.

Hermán pointed at the first and nodded, shook his head at the second, then pointed at himself.

Hostiles on the ground floor, friendlies above.

Hermán cleared his throat. When Darwin looked at him he made finger-and-thumb pistols, shot them like a cowboy, and pointed at the ground floor. "Office."

Darwin drew a rectangle in the dirt floor, then an X outside the lower left corner where they were. Hermán got it right away, made two squares on the inside corners. That put a long hallway on the other side of the double doors, rooms on both sides.

Hermán drew a thin line down the hall and turned into the left square before the corner. Then the letter L—no, a pistol.

His guns.

"Robbie?" Darwin said.

Hermán pointed to the second floor, indicated the far side, the front of the church. He drew that floor plan, so many lines and tiny rooms jumbled together Darwin lost track, finally patted him on the shoulder and said, "Let's go."

●●●

Darwin didn't like sending Hermán through the door first. He wanted to be the first one in, move and assess, clear the room. But it made sense for Hermán to take the lead, talk to anyone he saw and tell friendlies to get on the floor.

Hostiles, Darwin told him, just say hello.

Hermán opened the door on the right—Darwin next to him, crouched against the jamb of the left one—and took his time checking his boots for dirt. Darwin watched his eyes as they flicked up, checked the hallway.

No shock or surprise.

Hermán stepped inside and Darwin curled in behind him, put a hand on his back and poked the M4's suppressor over his shoulder. The hallway was dirty white walls and a wooden floor for about fifteen feet, two doors on the right and one on the left, all open, then it opened into the main room of the church.

It was dim but he could see the front doors straight ahead, also a double set but bigger and made of stained and carved wood instead of the plain ones behind him. Darwin closed the door to get rid of his silhouette. Men were talking somewhere ahead, no one in sight.

The closest door was on the right, three steps away, open. He could see the corner just inside the door, a faded painting of the Virgin Mary looking back at him. Darwin moved Hermán against the left side of the hallway and pressed a hand against his chest—stay put—then moved into the room with the M4 tracking counter-clockwise.

Far left corner clear.

Boarded window.

Far right corner clear.

Near right corner clear.

He flowed right along the wall to check around a busted-up desk, nobody. Books were lying on the desk and floor, papers scattered everywhere. A potted plant was tipped over near the window, gray soil spilled, the plant withered.

Darwin stood in the doorway and pointed at the door on the left, made a pistol and raised his eyebrows at Hermán, who nodded. Darwin pointed at the door on the right. Hermán mimed taking a leak, then mouthed that it was broken.

Darwin pointed at Hermán, used hand gestures to indicate what he wanted.

Hermán nodded and took a deep breath, walked down the hallway toward the men talking. He passed the door on the left and glanced inside.

"*Hola.*"

The men stopped talking and Darwin heard Rojo's voice: "Hey, take your time. You're lucky nobody shot you out there."

Hermán stopped. Darwin was pressed against the left wall, an inch from the doorway.

Keep going, Hermán.

"What's happening?" Hermán said.

"Don't worry about it, your garden is safe." Rojo.

Another man laughed. Two so far.

"Is my son okay?"

"We're about to go to war, old man, and your son is on the front line. Let us work."

"War?"

"Get the fuck out of here!" Not Rojo's voice. Maybe the laugher, maybe not.

Hermán's jaw clenched. "See you three later."

He turned and stepped out of the doorway and Darwin filled it. Straight ahead a large man was facing away, peering through a slit in the window boards. Darwin shot him in the back of the head.

He cycled left, past Rojo standing there behind a desk with his mouth open, to a man sitting next to a massive rack of assault weapons behind steel mesh. He had an M-16 with a grenade launcher across his lap. Darwin shot him twice in the chest and once in the face, came back and slammed the end of the suppressor into Rojo's forehead, knocked him back into an office chair.

Darwin stepped around the desk and kept the rifle pointed at his face. Rojo was big, bigger than Darwin. He had his hands up near his shoulders and his mouth hadn't closed yet.

"Where is Robbie?"

"Who the hell are you?"

Darwin tapped him again with the muzzle.

Rojo's eyes squeezed shut. His left hand rubbed his forehead, two round welts already red and swelling.

"Is he upstairs?"

Rojo kept one eye shut. "You the one got blood all over my truck?"

"That was Luis. Hermán, your guns are ready."

Hermán stepped in. "He has the key."

"Toss him the key," Darwin said.

"Fucking gardener. Come and get it."

Darwin kicked him in the belly, low, near his bladder. Air flew out and he almost tipped out of the chair. "Come take it Hermán. He resists I'll kill him."

Hermán stepped toward Rojo, hesitated, then leaned the big man to one side and rooted in his pocket. Came out with a keyring and went to the rack.

Rojo watched him. When he caught his breath he said, "Hermán, your son is going to die."

"No. I'm going to get him now. We're all going to get our families back. We're done with you."

"It's not us going to kill him," Rojo said. "It's Maro."

Staring at Darwin when he said it.

"Maro's out there trying to start a war. He's going to get everyone killed. Your son, all the workers. And this man's partner, and a woman. A Border agent."

He smiled, showed his gold tooth and asked Darwin, "You know about all this?"

•••

Cal worked through the rocks and scrub around the southeast side of the big hill, slipped over a ridge and there was the Rio below him. Across the water the land had that gentle slope and he could see the tower site and the blue Conex, maybe a half mile away, and past those the trailers and the red one at an even mile.

Shapes were running all over the place. He brought the rifle up and scoped it, watched the gestures and body language that made him think of one word: Frantic.

He scanned his side of the river, didn't see anyone and wasn't close enough to the northwest end of the hill to see if the guys carrying Gabe were coming around yet.

If they were.

They were. Had to. He pulled his phone and found the number Darwin had given him for the Border agents.

"Who's this?" Guy was out of breath, his voice sharp.

"This is Nilla, who am I speaking with?"

"Nilla?"

"Guy with the beard."

"Where the hell are you?"

"I'm working, is this Molina?"

"Yeah, is Anna with you?"

Cal said, "No."

"Well we can't find her. Everyone's accounted for but her and she isn't responding via radio. We're starting a sweep toward the river."

Cal sat down and propped the rifle on his knees, scoped the landscape over there for her. "What was her last location?"

"The trailers with me and Foster. We chased the shooters away, came back and she was gone. We got two civilians dead, man. The engineers are all half-deaf, talking about the cartels. It's a clusterfuck."

"Who's dead? Jim died?"

"No, the helo flew him out. Marty and his assistant, the Dave guy. You guys were supposed to be protecting them, where the fuck are you?"

Ah, shit. Gauntlet had never lost a client before, let alone the principle. Something to worry about and deal with later. Cal told Molina about the tunnel entrance and how Marty was the project lead on it, about Robbie, about Gabe getting snatched.

"Jesus," Molina said. "You think they grabbed Anna?"

"I don't know man. I'll watch for her."

"We got more people coming. Everybody's rolling."

"Good," Cal said, thinking: We need to wrap this up, get our asses over the border. He stashed the phone and moved across the slope toward the northwest end of the hill, scanning for threats, Gabe, and now Anna.

Cal stopped when he could see the northwest end of the hill. He found a good spot—concealment from the ridge above and fields of fire left, right, below—and surveyed the network of trails on the slope between him and the river.

Hard to tell from the new angle, but he figured he was right above the spot Darwin had pointed out, where the guy with the shovel had killed the farmer. Some of the trails snaked through the scrub and met at the base of the northwest slope, where the men carrying Gabe ought to show up.

He put the scope on that spot and got into a solid position, gun on bone on ground.

Come on.

Come on.

•••

Darwin told Hermán, "Go get Robbie."

Hermán stopped loading assault rifles and grabbed the M-16 out of the dead guy's lap, stepped to the hallway and checked both ways.

"Hermán."

He looked at Darwin.

"Don't shoot anybody with that yet. Any trouble, come back to me. Sing your song if everything is okay."

Hermán turned left into the hallway and was gone.

"He can't shoot anybody," Rojo said, still leaning back in his chair with his forehead turning purple. "He's a gardener."

"Tell me where Maro is."

"How would I know? I never do."

"He has my man with him?"

Rojo shrugged.

"You got him on that phone?"

"Sure, but he never answers. He keeps his off unless he needs to make a call. It's very irritating."

"Call him."

"You know we were loading up to go see him. You could have come with us, but instead you shot everybody."

"Not yet. Where were you going?"

"To the river."

"You mean the tunnel."

"Oh, you know about that, huh?" Rojo squinted, looked from the M4 pointed at his face to Darwin. "You tell anybody?"

"Call."

Rojo picked his phone up. "I hope you didn't tell anybody. The secret dies with you, good, but I have to go around for a bunch of people, man. That's a lot of work."

He punched a button and held the phone up. It started ringing on speaker, then clicked.

"You here already?"

211

"Maro?"

"Yes, what?"

Rojo shrugged and shook his head, shocked. "I didn't think you'd answer."

"You change your mind? You going to help me now?"

Darwin said, "Stop what you're doing and release my man."

The line hissed. "Rojo, who's there with you?"

"An American. A soldier."

"He's not a soldier, he's a babysitter. Sheepdog, is that you?"

Darwin said, "Stop what you're doing. Tell me where you are, I'll come get my man."

"I don't have your man, I have your woman."

"Bullshit."

"Is it?"

"Maro."

"Patrick."

Darwin could hear the grin through the phone. "I'm done fucking around with you. Whatever your plan is, it will not work. It will end badly for you."

"You should be helping me too. Men like us, we need wars. Bitches like Marty and Rojo, they need desks. Smash them up and use them for firewood on the battlefield, my friend."

Darwin took a breath. "Is my man still alive?"

"I don't know. I was about to call *my* man to see, but you two called first."

"I know he's wounded. Treat his injuries. Don't make it worse than it is. This church is taken. Your tunnel is dead. Maro, you have lost."

"See, you not listening. I don't give a fuck about the tunnel. You know I killed Marty and his puppy David? What does that tell you?"

Rojo closed his eyes.

Darwin stared at the phone. Marty and Dave? Anna? He

pushed it all aside, misinformation to keep him off balance.

Hermán's singing came down the hallway. Darwin saw him in the doorway with a skinny, pale man with blonde hair sticking up all over the place, blinking even in the dim light of the office. He looked away from the bodies and blood, stared at Darwin.

Darwin said, "Robbie?"

"Yeah."

"I'm here to take you home."

Into the phone: "Maro, I'll see you soon."

CHAPTER 22

DARWIN TOOK ROJO'S phone and stuffed it in a pocket. Saw the truck key on the desk, grabbed that too.

"Robbie, can you walk?"

"Yeah."

"Run?"

"I think so. I'm not hurt or anything, just been sitting a lot."

Hermán said, "Pardon me," squeezed past Robbie into the office and went back to work on the run rack, pulling and checking rifles then leaning them against the wall. "Robbie, let them through please. Come on everybody."

A line of men and women came through the door without a sound, filed past Hermán and took a weapon from him, then waited for a gap to step out into the hallway.

"You're all going to die," Rojo said.

"Shut up," Darwin said. To Hermán: "I need to leave."

"I know, but I don't think you can sneak away." He nodded at the window.

Darwin tried to see through the slits from his spot. No good. Told Rojo, "Don't move."

"I have him," a woman said. She was about thirty and pointed an AK at Rojo's chest.

Hermán put a hand on her shoulder. "Not yet."

Darwin stepped to the window. The look on the woman's face, she's only thought about this moment a million times. He peered through a slit and saw a dozen gunmen milling in the road on the other side of the garden and sandbagged wall.

"The same all around," Hermán said. "They don't know what to do until Rojo tells them."

Rojo dipped a nod, showed his gold tooth.

"So we will give them something to do," Hermán said.

Darwin said, "I can't stick around."

"Is okay, but if you can shoot anybody on your way out, that would help."

They shook hands.

Rojo said, "Christ."

Darwin walked Robbie into the main room of the church, a few pews left, either tipped over or shoved against the walls. The armed men and women stood next to the boarded windows, somber but ready.

More people came down out of a staircase in the corner and headed for the office. Everybody waved to Robbie. He waved back, told them, "I guess I'm leaving, thank you. Thank you."

Darwin put him next to the front doors and peered through a window. The truck was there facing the church—nose-out would be better, but what did he want, a valet? He could see a man's boots beneath the open driver's door. The guy was leaning into the cab, came out with a bloody rag and yelled something down the driveway to a few guys with assault rifles standing outside the open gate, trying to look serious.

They waved him off, shooed him back to work.

Darwin went to the door. He saw Hermán standing in the hallway outside the office. Gave him the thumbs-up. Hermán looked into the office and nodded.

Rojo's voice came out of the room: "Hey."

Robbie jumped when the AK fired, then covered his head and dropped to his knees when everybody in the church opened up, firing through the slits to pour it on the gunmen outside.

Darwin hauled him up and ripped the door open. The man at the truck stood there with an AR-15 in his hands, then someone in the church tore him apart with a burst.

Darwin walked with Robbie in a headlock to the passenger side of the truck, shoved him into the footwell and slammed the door. Ran around the front and got in, turned the key and had them spun around before the slugs started thumping into the sheet metal. No idea where they were coming from, dust and gunfire all around.

He floored the truck out of the dust cloud, stomped the brake as they went through the gates and cranked left into a semi-controlled slide, powered through that and jumped forward.

Gunmen were crouched along the wall, no idea what the fuck was going on. Some of them saw the truck and ran toward it, maybe thinking it was Rojo. Darwin blew past them, had the .45 ready in case anybody made it aboard. They vanished behind the truck in dust.

Darwin had to slow down going between the houses—on an actual road this time, sort of—weaving around piles of junk and lean-tos that crept into the space. He cleared the buildings and bounced through the ditch, peeled left and found the two-track he and Luis had used. Didn't slow down until they were out of the junkyard and over the ridge, even then kept the truck fast but not suicidal.

"Stay down there Robbie. You okay?"

"Yeah." He was braced between the seat and the glove box, getting jerked around with every bump. "Are they going to be okay back there?"

Darwin shrugged. "Sorry man. Fido."

"Fido?"

Darwin had his cell phone out. Cal hadn't called with new information—that was how he looked at it, as information, not good news or bad. As the call went through he thought, Yeah, then why you holding your breath?

Cal answered immediately. "Nilla."

"Sheepdog here, I have Robbie. How we doing?"

"This is bad, Sheepdog. This is real bad."

●●●

Cal watched through the scope, kept one ear on the phone and the other tuned into the hillside around him, kept his voice low. "Gabe's in bad shape. They've been rough on him, but he's moving."

"Where?" Darwin said, the sound of an engine and moving air in the background.

"In the scrub at the base of the ridge, northwest end. They're all hunkered underneath him like he's a tarp. They know someone's watching."

"Anybody out looking for you?"

"Not actively. Some guys standing on the hills around them, but nothing mobile. They were waiting for your buddy with the shovel to show up."

"Name's Maro."

"He has Anna."

Just the engine and air, then Darwin said, "Shit, I thought he was bluffing. He kill Marty and Dave too?"

"That's the story."

"This guy, man. Fuck it, we'll sort it out later."

"Roger. Anna's banged-up but walking. She looks pissed."

"I bet. What do you think?"

"No shot, man. Any of those donks is even half switched-on, I'll lose one or both of them."

"Listen, he isn't going to bargain with them," Darwin said, then ran down Maro's big plan.

"He sounds like a fucking lunatic. But you know what, it

might work. Very briefly and loudly."

"Even if it doesn't, Gabe and Anna are dead."

"Well. Anybody starts getting froggy down there I'll drop 'em, but we need another option."

"Can you see the blue Conex?"

Cal kept his eye on the scope but knew the shipper was squatting there across the Rio. "Affirmative."

"Anybody gone inside the tunnel since me?"

"I haven't had eyes-on the whole time, but don't believe so. I counted the Border agents running around the trailers, everyone's accounted for."

"It stays that way," Darwin said, then told him why.

"You've had a big day. Hey, they're up, they're moving. Walking Anna and carrying Gabe toward the river. Hurry up man, I'm looking at a fucking funeral procession here."

"I'm twenty minutes out, fast as I can go."

"I'm moving."

●●●

Cal wove downhill through the scrub, careful not to kick any big rocks loose and send them tumbling toward the river and anybody waiting down there.

The trail this guy Maro was on paralleled the river for a hundred yards—even had them looking straight in Cal's direction for twenty of them—then twisted and cut all the way to the shore, where the land was flat and sandy.

When they made that turn and showed him their backs, Maro out front with his AK in Anna's spine and the guys carrying Gabe trailing, Cal picked up the pace and moved toward them from their five o'clock. The wind was blowing south-southwest, into his face, carrying any sound he made away from the river.

He found a shallow gulley that shadowed the path, probably ran all the way to the water, thick brush on each side just like the one he'd found the grenade in. He dropped in and followed it, could hear the river ahead and men talking at his eleven o'clock. Not far, maybe thirty yards.

No good being downhill from them.

He started up the far side of the gulley, had his head and torso over the lip when the shot came, one round from the AK. Cal went flat, had the M4 ready but knew from the sound the shot hadn't come toward him.

A man started yelling—shit, Gabe calling for help—no, someone yelling across the Rio.

"Attention! Attention!"

Another shot.

Cal used the racket to cover his movement out of the gulley, got near the trail and found a mesquite trunk to kneel behind, the thing not even wide enough to cover his forearm, but better than nothing.

Through the scrub he could see the men holding Gabe, twenty yards away in a little clearing, facing the water. Now they had Gabe on his feet, a man on each side, his arms draped over their shoulders. A third knelt off to the far side of the trail, kept glancing the way they'd come.

Gabe's head drooped. The man who'd crouched underneath him was closer to the river, holding Anna by the hair.

Maro, shovel in one hand, was in front of everybody, his AK pointed at the sky.

"Hey over there," he said. Fired again.

Anna flinched. Gabe didn't.

Then Maro started walking into the Rio, five, ten feet, but didn't drop down past his calves.

The fuck?

Cal had swum across during the night, and ten feet in he couldn't touch bottom. There'd be various depths along the shore, but nothing like this. The guy was on some kind of structure, maybe a submerged rock?

Cal couldn't see the far side of the Rio but someone must have shown up.

"Finally," Maro yelled. "Hey, you out of breath? Take your time, I wait."

He turned and said something to his men, got a laugh.

Then he yelled across the Rio, "Okay, I want you to see something."

The man holding Anna shoved her toward Maro, kicked her legs out and held her on her knees. She tried to pull free, twist around and hit him. Maro punched her in the face and she sagged. The man with her hair had to hold her upright.

Maro yelled, "This is what happens when the United States fucks with the cartels."

He made a show of leaning his AK against a rock, held the shovel up for all to see. The man holding Anna moved away.

Cal burst onto the trail, stepped forward with the M4 up. The men holding Gabe were between him and Maro, Anna low to the ground. Cal shot both of the men in the back of the head. They dropped, pulled Gabe down with them onto his back.

Cal swept left and shot the man kneeling along the trail, the guy's gun still pointed at the dirt.

The man who'd held Anna was turning, bringing his rifle up, his face pinched. Cal was fifteen yards away, put two into his chest. He went for Maro last, the only one without a gun, but the guy was quick as a fucking snake.

Cal acquired him just as he darted away from the rock with his AK in hand and ducked behind Anna, pulled her to her feet and pressed the barrel to the base of her skull, stepped backward toward the Rio.

Cal kept moving forward.

"I'll shoot her," Maro said.

Cal didn't slow. He stepped over a dead man next to Gabe. "Hang on buddy." He cleared that pile and stopped ten feet from Anna. All he could see of Maro was bits of fatigues and the muzzle of his rifle. Not even a boot or elbow sticking out.

Cal yelled to whoever was standing there across the river, "If you have a shot, take it."

No way they would. If they decided to violate international laws and borders and shoot, it would probably go through Maro and hit Anna. Or miss and hit Cal. But get Maro thinking about it, maybe he'll show something worth shooting.

Cal stepped to his left, said, "Anna, can—"

He didn't hear the shot but felt it and knew that's what it was, had felt it before, a slug pounding into the thin armor across his back. He heard the second one that hit him behind the left shoulder as he was turning, looking for the shooter and didn't see anybody.

Then he saw Gabe holding a pistol, pointing it at him, shooting again and hitting him in the chest. Something slammed into his helmet from behind and he saw the sky, then nothing.

● ● ●

Maro shoved Anna all the way to the ground and looked at the man lying at his feet, this beast with weapons and equipment all over him. It looked like his armor had stopped the dinky pistol rounds, but hit him in the back of the head with the butt of the AK and sure enough, he goes down like anyone.

Maro kicked him to be sure, see if he'd grunt, but no, he was out.

Maro smiled at Arturo, sitting there in the dirt wearing the other security man's clothes, his face swollen and bloody but smiling too. "I guess it worked," Maro said.

Arturo looked at the *salvajes* strewn around them. "I suppose."

He'd dressed up like the security man in case Darwin or this one with the beard showed up to negotiate. Maro had pictured it—they'd ask for Anna and their man back, he'd pretend to think about it, be scared, and finally say okay, take them, just don't kill me. Here, use our bridge. Nice, isn't it?

Then halfway across the Rio Arturo would spring the trap, shoot the men dead and drag Anna back to Mexico for her execution.

That was all just in case they showed up, so it was good of Arturo to take the beating on something uncertain. Maro helped him to his feet.

"Did they break anything?"

"No, I'm fine. They're good at beatings though, for sure." He tested a tooth with his thumb.

Maro said, "Is too bad about these guys, but man, I never thought Darwin or his men would come out shooting like that, not saying anything."

"They killed Juan and Javi, left them in the cave. Who knows about the ones in the tunnel."

Maro nodded. "I talked to Rojo. Darwin shot Luis, is there causing all kinds of trouble."

"At the church?"

"I know, surprised me too."

"These men—hey, she's trying to get away."

Maro turned and saw Anna crawling toward the Rio, elbows digging into the sand to drag the rest of her body.

"Hey, come on, you're getting all wet again."

He and Arturo pulled her back onto shore and stood over the man with the beard.

"This is good," Maro said. He waved to the Border agents standing on the American shore, most of them with binoculars and rifles, but only the binoculars were pointed at him. A couple were on radios or phones.

He listened, didn't hear any helicopters coming. Not that it mattered.

"Tell them to bring the other one out."

CHAPTER 23

DARWIN HAD HEARD the single shots from an AK when he and Robbie were still in the truck, just coming into the nest of bunkers and caves. He slid to a stop at the mouth of the cave with the tunnel entrance, dust rolling over the truck as he pulled Robbie across the seat and out the driver's door, kept him close and low as they moved into the cave.

No workers or gunmen around but the two dead men were still on the ground where he'd left them, just like the pallets and boards blocking the tunnel. Workers had the day off so far.

He asked Robbie, "You okay?"

"Yeah, just tell me what to do."

Then Darwin heard the faint pistol shots. One-two, three, then nothing.

Came from the other side of the big hill, near the river. He tried the throat mic, maybe in range, clicked it once to see if Cal would come back.

Nothing.

He didn't bother with the cell phone—if Cal was in a firefight, he'd be too busy to answer.

Darwin pulled Robbie to the trail that wrapped around the northwest end of the hill. "Keep up, stay behind me. Don't get shot."

"Ah, man."

Darwin checked all directions with the M4. The hills bumping up on the left bothered him. Rocks and scrub that could hide shooters, some of the clumps big enough to tuck a Jeep into.

He had that feeling, that pressure right before the action rolled.

Yeah, it's already rolling for everybody else—you need to catch up.

They wrapped around a bend to the right and had a straight trail ahead, looked like it ran parallel to the Rio for about a hundred yards. Halfway along, facing away, were two men with assault rifles and a man in his skivvies, bare feet, his hands bound behind his back and blood caked on the right side of his neck and back. He had a cloth wrapped around his head acting as a bandage and a blindfold. The gunmen were shoving Gabe along, making him hurry across the hot sand and rocks toward the next turn in the trail.

Darwin put a hand on Robbie's chest—stay put—and moved forward. He kept his eyes on Gabe, didn't want the gunmen to feel him staring at their backs. They were slow, had to keep pace with Gabe's shuffling. When Darwin was ten yards away the one on the left started to turn.

Darwin kept walking forward and shot him in the ear, turned and shot the other one in the back of the head.

"Poppa, it's Sheepdog. I got you."

"Jesus man, thank God." Gabe sagged against him. "My girls, man. My girls."

"You'll see them soon. Blindfold coming off." He waved Robbie up and pulled the dirty t-shirt off Gabe's head, stepped around to examine the wound. "All right bud, you're good to go."

"How bad?"

"Looks like a bullet skimmed up your neck and took a chunk outta your ear. No more matching earrings for you and your wife."

"Shit." Gabe smiled, showed his perfect teeth.

"Good to see that again," Darwin said. "You can walk? Everything working?"

"They tossed me around a bit but I'm good. Fucking assholes."

"Nilla is somewhere ahead. We got unknown hostiles holding Anna, the Border agent. Shots have been fired."

"I heard those," Gabe said. He picked up one of the rifles, an AR-15, checked the chamber and pulled an extra magazine out of a dead guy's thigh pocket.

Darwin checked him out. "You look like an episode of COPS. Hang back and cover Robbie, I'll take point."

Gabe looked at the engineer. "I take it you're Robbie."

"Yes sir."

"Stick close and don't mind the blood. Only makes me stronger."

•••

Darwin took the lead, moved ahead to the turn that went left toward the Rio. He checked the corner and saw it stayed flat for a bit then dropped—all he could see was a horizon about twenty yards away. He moved to that in a crouch. Gabe and Robbie stayed at the turn, Gabe scanning all directions.

Darwin took a peek over the edge and could see all the way to the river, the scene breaking into sections as he took it in:

A clearing on the shore, Maro standing with his AK pointed at the sky.

Anna lying face-down in the wet sand.

Cal lying on his side, half in the river.

A man in bloody and dirty clothes standing over Cal with a chrome revolver in his hand, pointed at Cal.

Darwin was aiming while he processed this, had the man with the pistol lined up when Maro looked up the trail and dove toward Anna, no hesitation.

Darwin fired and saw the pistol man's head come apart. His body dropped onto Cal, rolled Cal further into the water where the current grabbed his leg and started tugging him downstream.

Darwin was up and moving toward Maro, now crouched behind Anna and yanking her by the hair to keep her on her knees, the rifle pressed into her jawline.

Anna looked half out of it, one eye swollen shut and the other glassy and rolling. It found Darwin and cleared up, widened. She open her mouth to talk, then the eye drifted away and almost closed. Tears ran out of it over her jaw, the muscles there clenched into knots.

Maro pulled her all the way up and backed toward the river, then side-stepped enough to kick Cal all the way into the water.

Cal spun face-up in the current, turned over and went under.

Maro side-stepped again and backed into the river but didn't drop into the water.

Darwin stopped a few feet from the edge, the M4 aimed and ready for even a sliver.

"I'm getting tired of this," Maro said.

"Then show me your face."

"Your man is sinking, floating away."

"I'll find him."

"He isn't dead yet, you gonna let him drown?"

"He's a decent swimmer."

"I see the other one behind you. Tell him to put his gun down and come to the water."

"No."

"I'll shoot her."

"And I'll shoot you. You won't get to enjoy your own little war."

"Little?" Maro said. "I don't think so my friend. I want big."

"You been at war with two of us since midnight, no air support, intel, or artillery. How's it going so far?"

"I killed Marty and Dave. Your babies."

"Traitors. And you know what? They fired me. I think I'll sleep okay."

"I kill this one, how about then?"

"Do not."

"It's happening."

Darwin scanned for a shot, any shot, or a way to signal the Border agents on the far shore—do something to get break this guy loose. Then his earpiece clicked.

Cal said, "I'm in the middle of the river, forty yards downstream. No weapons. Make it fast, I'm in bad shape here."

Darwin glanced that way, saw a tangle of trees and branches hung up in the river with a lump about the same shape as Cal's head. He said to Maro, "You want big, kill a decorated veteran of the United States military."

"I think I just did that."

"The way you wanted? With your little shovel there?"

The green tool with its sharp edges was lying on the shore a few yards away.

"Tell me what you saying."

"You know I'll kill you if you shoot her. You know it. Let her go. Let my man and Robbie go."

"And I get you?"

"Yup."

"I gonna chop your head off."

"You wanna talk about it or do it?"

•••

Gabe and Robbie walked to the shore, unarmed. Darwin still had the M4 waiting for Maro to show something, but he wasn't holding his breath.

Gabe stopped next to Darwin. "Sheepdog, the hell you doing?"

"Go on man. All good here."

Gabe didn't move, waited for some kind of sign what to do.

"Just go man. I got this. Get home to your girls."

Gabe turned toward the river. He and Robbie stepped onto the submerged bridge Maro and Anna were on.

Darwin thought, Man, it's killing him.

Flip the roles, how would you feel? Couldn't imagine.

"In the water," Maro said. He didn't move, made Gabe and Robbie get into the river and swim on the downstream side of the bridge where the rip current pulled them hard.

"Okay," Maro said. "Let's go before your man gets to the other side and has the balls to shoot at me. Put your weapons down."

"You gonna shoot me?"

"Hey, you ask for the *saperka*, that's what you get."

Darwin tossed the M4 into the bushes, pulled the .45 and did the same.

"What else? Knives? You got a shotgun in your pocket?"

"Turn her loose," Darwin said.

"Get on your knees."

Here we go. He comes around her with that AK, this will officially be the dumbest thing you've ever done. He dropped to his knees, felt them pop and groan.

Maro finally peeked over Anna's shoulder, grinned at him and stepped into the open. "Ta dah!"

Anna came to life, screamed and turned into Maro, tried to club him with a fist. Maro looked shocked for half a second, took the blow on his shoulder and swept her aside, dumped her into the Rio with the muzzle of his AK.

She howled, fought the current to get back at him while he looked from her to Darwin, the rifle aimed center-mass, shook his head and smiled.

Anna ran out of gas. Her swollen face dipped below the surface once, again. She bobbed downstream, sputtering, "I'm so sorry. So sorry."

"She's sorry," Maro said. He had his full attention on Darwin now and didn't see Cal's arm come out of the river to snag Anna, then the two of them plowing across the current toward Texas, Cal still strong enough to keep them both moving and breathing.

Maro stepped to the shore and plucked the shovel out of the sand, moved back into the Rio and rinsed the grit off the blade. He slung the AK over his head and spun it behind him.

"Well. It's time, Sheepdog."

"I'd like to call my wife."

Maro frowned. "Your wife? Man, you are a dog, the way you been going after my Anna. I saw you two, don't lie."

Darwin put a hand on his pouch.

Maro touched the AK.

"Just a phone," Darwin said.

"You gonna let me talk to her? Tell her I gave you a chance to be a man again, a warrior, but you not interested."

Darwin took his cell phone out. "I think she'd be surprised to hear that."

"Hey, tell her to stay on the line and see if she can record this next part. They play it on the news channels, the sound of you dying on your knees. It could help me out. You have video on that?"

"No." He found the right number.

"Is too bad. Hey, hurry up, your guys are on the shore."

Darwin checked, saw Gabe and Robbie on the far side, Border agents rushing toward them and Cal and Anna, further downstream and just stepping out of the water.

"Hey, he was alive," Maro said. He shrugged, said to

Darwin, "Maybe I see him on the battlefield, we tell some stories about you."

"This one's my favorite," Darwin said, and called Gabe's company cell phone. It was sitting outside the cave under the burlap, wired to a blasting cap and the det cord. When the blasting cap blew the cord took off like a rocket, zipped into the tunnel entrance and underground all the way to the dynamite he'd packed into the supports.

The earth jumped a couple inches and shook. Downstream and across the river a line of dust and rocks burst into the air, ran all the way to the tower site. Darwin couldn't see the blue Conex but heard it pop into the air and crash back down, a plume of dust mushrooming over the landscape.

Maro flinched and ducked and stared, his mouth open, and Darwin was up onto one knee moving toward him when the bridge collapsed, the sand and gravel pulled downstream, the exposed tunnel like a vacuum pulling all the water in.

One second Maro was there, Darwin reaching and wanting to tear him apart, the next he was gone. He disappeared into the brown water, sticks and rocks and steel tubing getting broken and bent from the force of the water.

Darwin thought he saw a severed hand holding a *saperka* get churned up and sucked back under, but it could have been a tree root.

CHAPTER 24

DARWIN SAT ON the steps to their trailer with a towel around his neck. He was still damp from his swim after the river had calmed down, wanted to get out of the heavy clothes.

Border agents worked on Cal, Gabe, and Anna, the first aid kits dumped in a pile for easy access to the gauze and pads. Anna broke loose and limped over with a blue ice pack pressed against her eye.

"Welcome to Texas."

Darwin smiled. "Thanks, I hear the food's great."

"Hey, you never got to eat the dinner I brought you."

"I had a few bites."

"Well, either way, I owe you a couple beers. Every day for life."

"How you feeling?"

She sat on the step next to him. "My face hurts. Molina says I have a concussion, same as Cal."

They looked over at him, sitting in the sun with his shirt off so Molina could look at the massive welts and bruising from the pistol slugs.

Molina told him, "I mean it man, you can't fall asleep."

"I heard you," Cal said. He yawned and started taking his boots off.

Gabe was on the phone with his wife and daughters, laughing and crying and posing for the agents cleaning the cuts and abrasions he had just about everywhere.

"I think my pride hurts the most though," Anna said. "Guy took me down. Last thing I remember clearly is talking to you outside Marty's trailer. The whole time I was, what, a hostage? *Me*? I had no idea what was going on. Even in the river, I thought I was winning."

Darwin shook his head. "He was a highly skilled enemy with a specific plan of action. Guys like him can stop entire armies, so don't beat yourself up."

"You took him out."

"Yeah, with a shit-ton of dynamite and the forces of nature."

"How'd you blow that tunnel?"

"Any of this admissible in a court of law?"

"Hey, you don't have the right to remain silent right now. I gotta hear this."

Darwin told her.

"Jesus. How'd you get your phone out?"

Here we go. "Told him I wanted to call my wife."

"Your wife."

"Yeah."

"Is this wife real?"

"Most of the time."

"Huh."

They were quiet for a while, then Anna said, "Kinda feel like I got gut-punched again."

"Yeah, I'm sorry about that."

"What's her name?"

"She has her way, it won't be Darwin much longer."

"Interesting. When that happens, let me know. We'll get those beers. And I still get to shoot that gun of yours."

"Deal. These beers gonna be in prison?"

"Prison—for what, being kind of an asshole?"

"You know."

Anna moved the ice pack from her eye to her head. "Oof, that hurts. I talked to my guys. Our report will show a hostile border crossing into Texas, likely a rival to the Luna Cartel. Gunmen killed Marty and Dave, destroyed a tunnel, and engaged in a firefight with Luna gunmen and Border agents. Civilian contractors assisted but were not primary factors."

"I'm not asking you to lie for us—"

"I don't care. It's done."

"I was gonna say, but I really appreciate it."

Anna said, "You want to see Marty and Dave?"

"Nah. I know what it looks like."

"That can't be a good thing, your clients getting killed."

"Nope."

"What happens, you lose your job?"

"We'll see. I'll tell the boss everything, see what shakes out."

"Everything."

Darwin shrugged. "The way we work. He can keep a secret."

"Your men are okay with all this?"

"We'll do a hot wash, talk about what went wrong. Gabe has some decisions to make. He got a close look at never seeing his family again. Cal, look at him. He's already making a list of who to show the scars to."

"Lot of strip clubs in Texas."

"You better warn them all."

"What about you?"

Darwin stood up, winced when his knees crackled. "We were all coming stateside for vacation. I think it's time for that. And I guess I should go call my wife. For real."

"Anything going to blow up this time?"

"Just about every time. You might want to duck."

FROM THE AUTHOR

I hope you enjoyed FIND > FIX > FINISH. I had a great time with these characters and look forward to the next adventure with Sheepdog and his fellow contractors.
For the latest information on my books, please visit www.jeremywbrown.com.
Thanks for reading,
Jeremy

Other books by Jeremy Brown:

Suckerpunch: Woodshed Wallace Series Round 1
Hook & Shoot: Woodshed Wallace Series Round 2
Anaconda Choke: Woodshed Wallace Series Round 3 (2014)
Show No Teeth (Murder Mystery)
The Kalamazoo Kid (Crime Thriller)
Crime Files - Four-Minute Forensic Mysteries: Body of Evidence
Crime Files - Four-Minute Forensic Mysteries: Shadow of Doubt